The Legend
of the
Missouri
Mud Monster

Also by Thomas L. Tedrow

The Younguns/Book Four

The Legend of the Missouri Mud Monster

❖

Thomas L. Tedrow

THOMAS NELSON PUBLISHERS
Nashville • Atlanta • London • Vancouver

To my family. Yesterday, today, forever.

Contents

Prologue

Natural forces that shaped Missouri's landscape blessed the Ozarks with thick forests, winding hollows, steep cliffs, and prominent peaks that stood out in the distance. A wonderland of nature's magic. A timeless world shaped only by the wear of the ages.

Caves, sinkholes, fresh springs, and clear streams were sprinkled through wooded, rolling hills filled with game. Panthers and wildcats roamed along with sheep-killing wolves, deer, bears, and small animals of every description.

Some defied description according to the legends. The Indians who once called the land their own spoke in hushed whispers about a half man, half beast who roamed the land. Early settlers heard the stories and saw the strange tracks. They called it the Mud Monster, and it was the stuff of nightmares.

They said it would come walking out of the shadows on the nights when you heard the floorboards creak. When the wind would shrill down your chimney or blow the flap open on your tent. Hovering by the stove, hoping that the glowing, red-lantern coals would protect them, the people of the Ozarks who believed in the legend would swear that they could smell his stink. Like a dank river or a decayed pond, the tall, hairy creature was waiting out there. Waiting to grab their livestock and any hapless child unlucky enough to be outside when the monster passed by.

Mud Monster. Wildfire for the imagination. Some believed and some didn't. This is a story about strange tracks in the woods and a town that didn't see the monster walking among them.

Monster Tracks

❖

The tracks he'd been following weren't human. They were something else. He was a good judge of tracks. Read them like a school-taught man reads books. All Henry Mead could think about were the Mud Monster legends he'd heard whispered over campfires as a boy. Stories of a half man, half beast that loped through the woods, carrying off naughty children. Even though the old man was two moons shy of seventy, the old haunts still brought back chills.

He looked down at the tracks that led to the spring-fed watering hole. The creature had come this way. Even with his half good eyes Henry Mead was sure the tracks were morning fresh. Still, he was puzzled. He thought he had seen just about everything. But this was different. The tracks just stopped. The humanlike prints came to an end. Like the creature had taken off into the air.

But there was no sign of the old man's floppy-eared dog. His howling had stopped a half hour back.

"Rufus, come back, boy," he drawled out.

Ru-fusssss. Ru-fusssss. Ru-fusssss. His echo bounced off the ravine.

Pushing back his glossy silver hair that hung from the widow's peak on his large forehead, Henry Mead recognized raccoon and opossum, fox and gray squirrel tracks from ealier visitors to the site. There was even a set of skunk prints that a weasel had all but scratched out. An owl had left just one print and the remains of the mouse it had eaten.

Ants were already picking the bones. But Mead couldn't find any more monster prints.

"Must have lost the trail back at the rocky ridge." Then, looking down, he saw the paw prints of his dog Rufus as clear as day.

"Rufus, come here, boy." Mead looked around, hopeful. "Rufus, come on back now."

Now, now, now, echoed back. He finger-whistled. Clapped his hands. The woods absorbed all sound. Nothing answered but the deep sounds of the Ozarks. Nothing. It was as if Rufus had disappeared.

Mud Monster creeps up and grabs you. Pulls you by the hair. Bites your head off.

Mead took cautious steps, trying to block out the campfire tale that was right behind his eyes. It was eerie and getting early-dark. The air smelled of rain. A three-foot opossum scurried toward the watering hole then stopped. He watched the strange, rat-looking animal flex. The thumbs on its hind feet moved in opposite directions, its prehensile tail curled back and forth. It looked at Mead, wondering if the human meant danger. Then, finding a toad, the opossum chewed it quickly. Mead shifted his weight, scaring the opossum, which backed up, releasing a pungent odor to defend itself.

"Go on, git," he said, holding his nose until he'd passed by the stink.

Mead stepped carefully, examining the ground for clues, looking through the early fallen leaves, trying to make sense out of what he was seeing. Rufus's tracks spun in circles. Like he'd been jumping in the air, trying to grab something. "This don't make sense," he mumbled, looking down, then up. There was nothing above him except the low-hanging tree branch. Turning to push the bushes and branch away, he looked around for more tracks, but the branch swung back, covering his face with an intricate spider web that stretched a dozen feet. Pulling the strings off his face, he saw the huge spider not two inches away, moving toward his bent nose that was a mirror reminder of a bar fight best left forgotten. The old man backed away, picking and pulling to get the web off his face.

Where's Rufus? he worried, picking at the mosquito welts on his arm.

"Should have never listened to that old Indian tell me 'bout the Mud Monster. Never. Scared me then and it scares me now," he grumbled, looking at the gray-black, rain-filled clouds moving over the Ozarks.

2

Old Faithful

❖

Terry loved mornings—hearing the rooster crow and Crab Apple, the mule, braying reveille. The auburn-haired eight-year-old Youngun boy sat on the third hole of the three-hole privy they called Old Faithful, a rabbit's foot dangling from his belt loop.

"Tell the sheriff that Red's in town," he shouted, riding his pretend privy horse across the range. "Tell him that I've come to rob the candy store."

His brother called out from the house for Terry to come back and help with the dishes, but Terry ignored him. With their father sick, everyone was supposed to pull an extra load. Terry knew he should— even told himself that he would—but work in general wasn't one of Terry's druthers. He'd rather spend his time playing in the privy than drying dishes.

"Gonna be a cowboy," he sang to himself, rocking back and forth on his imaginary horse. Though he had checked for snakes before he dropped his britches, he kept a close eye for anything crawling around.

It was a glorious morning after a great night of sawing logs. His eleven-year-old brother Larry and his six-year-old sister Sherry were working and he had once again used the call of nature as an excuse to get out of his chores.

The privy was the one place where he could keep from doing chores. His father would throw up his hands in exasperation every time Terry said he felt the call after dinner—just when the dishes needed drying.

Terry didn't know where his sister was, but he wasn't talking to her anyway. As a matter of fact, he'd pledged to the world that he'd never speak to her again. It was a pledge he routinely made and broke each week, but it felt good each time he said it.

"Take that, you rustler!" Terry shouted, shooting his finger gun.

Dangit the dog poked his nose around the door, wondering what the ruckus was about. "Get out, wolf!" Terry shouted.

Dangit wasn't a wolf, but when Terry's imagination was at work he was whatever beast Terry wanted him to be. Dangit was really just a mutt. A lazy mutt without much hair, a spot on his head, and he would rip the cuff from your pants if you used his name in anger.

The dog stuck his head back in. "Get ready for a third eye!" Terry grinned, pretending to shoot a hole between the dog's eyes.

Dangit cocked his head, unable to figure out his squirrelly master. So he turned around and went back to digging foxholes in the yard, so he could either jump out at blue jays or just lie on his back when it got a bit hotter, four paws sticking in the air, waiting for nothing except a friendly pat.

"That dog sneaks in again, I'm gonna tie him up and let ol' Ratz the cat throw up a hairball on him," Terry mumbled. He didn't hear his sister sneak up. Sherry crept forward, trying not to giggle. She was wearing an old burlap sack with eyeholes cut out, looking like a country ghost. She scratched at the side of the privy with a stick, moving the sack so she could see better.

Rap, rap, rap.

"Who's there?" Terry called out, wondering if he should pull his trousers up.

Rap, rap, rap.

Sherry pulled the stick along the wooden ribs of the privy, growling in the deepest voice she could muster.

Rap, rap, rap.

She began pounding on the walls, howling wildly like a wolf.

Terry stumbled out of the privy with his undies half up and his pants down around his ankles. Sherry jumped out screaming, and Terry went running off faster than a tomcat up a tree. Sherry chased him, whooping and hollering until her brother stumbled and tumbled down into the grass. She pulled the sack off and doubled over with giggles.

"I'm gonna pound you," he muttered, tugging up his pants. He chased her across the yard, through the barn, over the fence, stumbled into Dangit's foxhole, then across the hog pen. Dangit followed, woofing and howling, part of the fun.

"Help me, Pa!" Sherry screamed, but they were too far away from the house and their father was too sick to do much of anything.

Squirrels dashed up their trees, Crab Apple the mule hee-hawed up a storm, and Bessie the pig all but drowned in the mud as the chase went on. TR the turkey—named for the former president—lost a bunch of feathers, and Bashful the fainting goat passed out when they crashed back through the barn, but the race didn't stop until Terry had Sherry cornered down by the creek.

"Say your prayers," he said, moving a step closer, his fist ready to land a good one. Dangit woofed him on, having a grand old time.

"Leave me alone!" Sherry shouted.

"Get ready to swim."

Edgar Allan Crow, the bird who lived in the barn, dive-bombed around them. But Terry wouldn't be put off.

"Help!" Sherry yelled.

"Dangit, what's Red and sis doin' now?" Maurice Springer, their neighbor, exclaimed as he walked up the path to the Younguns' house.

"Uh-oh," Terry said, hoping Dangit hadn't heard Maurice abuse his name. But he had.

Dangit raced toward Maurice's pant leg. His nose was almost touching the ground, his mouth wide open, full of teeth.

"Terry, stop him!" Maurice shouted. "Back, dog, back!"

Terry grabbed the dog by the tail just as he latched on to the ebony man's pant leg. "Let go, Dangit, let go!" Terry commanded.

Dangit was determined to rip the cuff off Maurice's pants for using his name in vain, but Terry managed to pull him away and scoot him back toward the house.

"Fool dog," Maurice grumbled.

Sherry tried to sneak away from her brother, but he cornered her again. She raced over and hugged Maurice's legs. "Don't let him hurt me. I was doin' nothin' and he 'tacked me."

"She tried to give me a heart 'tack in the privy," Terry said, reaching out to grab her dress.

"She did?" Maurice grinned, lifting the girl above his head. He pinched her button nose and pushed her sun-brown hair from her eyes.

Terry jumped up and down but couldn't reach her. "That's right. Pa says the privy's off-limits to such things."

"I only banged a stick and pre-ten-did to be a wolf," Sherry smirked.

"Well, bully for you but you done upset little Red here," Maurice said.

"Sorry," she whispered, snuggling up against Maurice's shoulders, locking her fingers onto his hand.

"Ain't right what she done," Terry said, stomping his feet. "Privies are for private biz-ness. You ought to make her go suck an egg."

"Like you never done nothin' to no one in that privy," Maurice said. "What 'bout that time you put the snake in there when Sherry was doin' her bizness?"

"I was too young to know better."

"Uh-huh. That was last week. And what about that time you shook that can of rocks, screamin' that a giant rattler was gonna get her if she didn't give you all her candy?"

"I was just funnin'. Weren't no such thing as a giant rattler. She was too dumb to know better."

"Now come on you two, I'm gonna go check on your pa and see how he's doin'."

Sherry's face puckered up. "Why won't he get better?"

"He'll get better," Maurice said. "Sometime's the body jus' needs time and rest." He looked at Terry. "You kids been helpin' out?"

"I been workin' so hard that I had to go sit in the privy to rest. Thought I was gonna have me a heart 'tack," Terry answered quickly.

Maurice shook his head. "Boy, I think you're slicin' the bologna too thin this time."

"Mr. Springer, are you and Mrs. Springer goin' to town tomorrow?" Sherry asked.

"Certainly girl, certainly. And if your pa don't mind, we're gonna ride over and take you kids with us in the wagon to town."

"To buy us candy?" Terry asked excitedly.

"You got any money?" Maurice said in a serious tone.

"I do," Sherry beamed.

"Good, then you'll get candy and your brothers can watch."

"Ain't fair," Terry grumbled. "She ought to share."

"Since when do you know anythin' 'bout sharin'?" Maurice asked.

Terry followed behind his sister, scheming a way to get the candy she hadn't even bought yet.

Where's Rufus?

❖

Rufus had been crazed for days, wanting to make a run at the creature that had been sneaking around the garbage pit behind the barn. The dog barked like he was fighting off the end of the world.

That should have been warning enough, but Mead was curious as to what this thing was. He had not seen it clearly, but whatever was coming around his property, it *wasn't* from the Ozarks. That should have been his first warning to leave well enough alone.

It also smelled bad, which should have been another warning. Sour milk bad. Like the devil stink the traveling tent minister had warned about. Every time the creature's awful smell drifted across the farm and into the kitchen, Mead had to lock Rufus up to keep him from tearing off through the woods in pursuit. *Rufus never backed down from nothin'. Shoulda figured he'd jump the pen to fight the thing. That ol' dog ain't scared of nothin'.*

Ever since he'd first caught glimpses of the man-thing poking through his trash, Mead couldn't resist trying to catch another peek at it. It would have been better if he hadn't lost his glasses, but it was still strangely wonderful to see something unknown running around behind the barn. Fascinated by the hairy creature that ran on its hind legs, Mead began leaving out different foods to see what it would eat.

He should have told the sheriff, but Mead was a solitary man who spent most of his time talking to himself. The only person he told was a kid at the orphanage when he was doing some carpentry work. At night he could hear the creature hooting out different calls which Mead tried to imitate, hooting back. But the creature got too friendly, hearing the man hoot back. Within a few days it tried to get into Mead's weather-beaten, clapboard house, thumping and shoving against the door, trying to get inside. If Rufus had not jumped the pen and taken off in a rush to follow the creature, Mead would have let it be. He would have stopped feeding it and fired his rifle into the air to drive it away. But Rufus had gone crazy, howling after the stinking thing. Mead had no choice but to follow after his faithful hound, listening to the drawn-out "boo-o-o-o" grow further and further away.

Now he was chasing the living ghost of the thousand Indian whispers. Mead shaded his cloudy eyes to the last red fading fast from the sky, looking off toward the tree-topped horizon. Even a city slicker could smell the rain in the air, Mead figured. He stopped to rest, leaning on a stubby pine, then went up the rocky ridge.

"Rufus, can you hear me, boy?" he called. Cocking his head hopefully to hear any distant baying, he closed his eyes, knowing that in spite of his optimism something was wrong.

Guess Rufus treed the thing. Maybe he's got it cornered and is waitin' for me up ahead.

He really didn't believe it, but false hope had a way of making a person grasp for straws in the wind. The only thing he really knew was that it was silent—deathly silent—and that Rufus had followed the Mud Monster, which could be anywhere. Anywhere.

Climbing, crawling, slipping, Mead made it up to a rock overhang which sheltered the pinprick rain drops. Wiping the water from his eyes, he looked out, seeing nothing but blue-gray rain falling in blinding sheets.

Black darkness came quickly, along with the rain. The stars and moon had been flooded from the sky. The old man looked around, worried, knowing he had gone too far to head back tonight, and it was too wet to make a comforting fire. He'd have to sleep wedged between the rocks like a lizard and wait until the morning to find his dog.

The wet-dark painted disturbing pictures in his mind—Mud Monster stories that his folks had told him to keep him in line. Fears that he'd hidden from under the covers that never seemed to go away. That were still on his mind.

Hope the creature don't come lookin' for me in the dead of night.
Thunder boomed. *Ain't real anyway. Stories were just made up.*

Mead shivered, trying to forget the bad dreams and at the same time
remember long-forgotten little-boy prayers. Lightning danced across
the horizon. Psalms wouldn't come to mind. The wet-dark clutched
him. Held him. The words to the Lord's Prayer stopped after the first
line. Mud Monsters, boogeymen, and wood witches came. They were
alive in his mind.

Mead's eyes followed the moon's path through the wet clouds,
counting off an hour's time. The stars hung low, dripping through the
mist. It was a dark, late night. He was uncomfortable against the rocks.
He was wet. His bones ached with arthritis.

Memories of another fearful night sixty years earlier came to Mead
as he lay hidden behind the rocks. Of a time when he had gone to the
old Indian's shack by the marsh to hear tales of the woods.

*He took me to the old graves. Hid way back in the woods. Four pole
burial spots, sapling scaffoldin' still lashed tight with rawhide ties.
Leaf-covered old skeletons wrapped in animal skins, waitin' for the
spirit world to take them.*

They'd made a fire that night by the Indian graves. Mead knew that
the Indians had lived in the Ozarks a lot longer than the whites and
understood things that weren't written in any books. He sat with the
old man, admiring his penny-bronze skin, waiting to hear how the Mud
Monster of the Ozarks came to be. To hear the stories the Indians
whispered in the dark of their winter lodges.

Mead remembered looking again at the Indian bodies high in the air,
hearing a wolf somewhere off in the distance, then running home
through the woods, afraid that the shape changer, the Mud Monster,
was after him.

Sixty years later he was still afraid.

4

Terry's Dinner

❖

With Rev. Youngun too sick to cook and clean, the old maids of the Methodist Ladies Aid Society had been coming around, bringing covered plates of food and helping with the cleaning. They washed the kids' clothes, brushed Sherry's hair, and made sure there was a full pantry of food.

On the nights that they didn't come, the Youngun kids took turns making dinner. Larry had gotten pretty good, and Sherry knew how to heat up leftovers, but Terry's cooking was downright awful. It was worse than worse. The only living thing that would eat it without complaining was Dangit the dog, who hid under the counter waiting for Terry to drop something.

"Kids shouldn't have to cook," Terry grumbled, looking at the plucked chicken that had been left for them to cook.

He lifted up the chicken, looking at it from both ends. "Makes you lose your ap-pee-tite when you see where they be comin' and goin'."

Tossing the chicken into the deep sink, he called out for his sister. "Sherry, come here quick, I need help."

Sherry strolled into the kitchen, knowing her brother was up to something. "What is it?"

"I'm feelin' bad. Think I got the runs. Would you just cook up Mister Chicken so I can go sit on the privy?"

"No."

"Pleeeeease!" he moaned, crossing his legs.

"Hundred times no. It's your turn to cook," she said, going back to her room.

He picked up the chicken. "Why you have to go and die all naked and pink on me like that? Least you coulda done was die like fried chicken. Why didn't you just die in the fryin' pan?"

"When's dinner?" Larry called out.

"When the sun freezes over," Terry called back.

Larry stuck his head in the kitchen. "Pa says he's not hungry, but I am."

"Eat this," Terry said, tossing the chicken across the room.

"Hey, watch it!" Larry shouted as the bird landed on the floor. Dangit was up off his feet before you could snap a finger. The dog grabbed the chicken by the foot and hightailed it out to the barn.

"That was our dinner," Larry complained.

"I'm tired of chicken anyway," Terry said.

"What you gonna cook up?"

"I'll think of something. Don't you worry." Terry knew he had to scheme his way out of cooking. "My stomach is hurtin' awful bad. You cook tonight. I need to go sit on the privy."

"I ain't fallin' for that line no more."

Terry shrugged. It was worth a try. "How come all these ladies are comin' round, worryin' after Pa?"

"Mr. Springer says that all the old biddies are lookin' for a husband."

"You mean Pa?"

"Uh-huh. Mr. Springer said that ugly ladies are always thinkin' they should be the mama of the good-lookin' widower's kids."

Terry shook his head, thinking about homely Miss Bruster. "You mean Pa would marry Miss Bruster? She looks like a string bean with a mop on her head."

"Just 'cause she likes Pa, don't mean he likes her," Larry answered.

"Why does he got to like anyone? We don't need a woman 'round here."

Larry shrugged. "Miss Janie Louis says that we need a good mama to take care of us."

"What does that old knobby-kneed crow know about kids? I bet she was birthed plain and ugly, came out jus' as she is now."

Larry agreed. Janie Louis was as plain as an old bucket. "You know what she told me?"

"What?"

"That she could go out at dawn and shoot a deer from two hundred yards, drag it back, dress it, and have venison steaks on the table that night for all of us."

"She better be careful goin' off into the woods. Someone might mistake her for a giant weasel and shoot her 'fore they knew any better."

"Don't be lettin' Pa hear you talkin' that way," Larry warned.

"If he thinks that coon-dog is pretty then I'll get him glasses. No-sir-ree, Pa don't need any woman fussin' 'round here when he's got us," Terry declared.

"Call me when dinner's ready."

Terry looked through the pantry and the vegetable bin, wondering what he could make that took the least effort. There was some salt pork in a barrel. A ham hung in the cold room. He also found a bunch of potatoes, carrots, and onions, which Terry wouldn't serve if it were the only food in the world. He hated carrots and wished the church ladies would quit bringing them by.

"Carrots should be 'gainst the law to eat." He heard Crab Apple the mule hee-haw out in the barn, and Terry made a quick trip out there, dropping all the carrots into his stall. "*You* eat them rabbit things."

Back in the kitchen, he decided that the best thing a cook could do was cook up something the cook liked to eat. "That's what I'm gonna do." Except that Terry had no intention of cooking. He pulled a kitchen chair into the pantry and took down the sugar bin. Then he set three bowls on the table and filled each one with sugar. Sticking a spoon in each, he called out loudly, "Dinner's ready."

Eulla Mae Springer stuck her head through the screen door and nearly scared Terry to death. "What you servin' up?" she asked.

"Oh, nothin'," he said, wondering how he was going to get out of this one.

"What you got three bowls of sugar sittin' on the table for?"

Terry didn't know what to say.

"Little Red, you mean you were servin' up bowls of sugar for dinner? What's gotten into you?" Eulla Mae exclaimed.

Maurice carried in two boxes of covered dishes. "Your pa told me that the church ladies weren't comin' tonight, so Eulla Mae thought she'd make you kids up some dinner."

5

Pa's Sick

❖

Before Eulla Mae left that night she cleaned the kitchen, prepared breakfast for the morning, and got the kids tucked into bed. Maurice got the barn in order, made sure all the animals had fresh feed and water, and then did a general check-over as best he could in the dark.

Rev. Youngun stayed upstairs in his room, drinking the herb tea that Eulla Mae had brought over and trying to finish the thick bowl of broth. When they went home, Rev. Youngun was left alone to worry.

Seven folks had died in the Ozarks from diphtheria in the past year. It wasn't an outbreak, wasn't a plague out of control, but it was walking death for children.

Rev. Youngun was sick. Whatever it was, it wouldn't let go. At first Dr. George had thought that diphtheria was what was ailing him. Then consumption. He ruled out yellow fever. Then decided it had to be a Chinese flu. He couldn't be sure because Rev. Youngun would be fine one day then down with a flulike fever the next. The medicine books weren't helpful, suggesting every kind of cure from vigorous horseback riding, to taking opium, to eating nothing but meat.

Rev. Youngun rocked in the dark, listening to the thunder. Sleeping was hard. The coughing spasms came without warning, doubling him up. He worried about choking to death, so he spent most nights sleeping sitting up. Thinking about Norma, wishing she hadn't died. Wondering what would happen to his three children if he didn't make it through this.

They've got no other living relatives. Except for Cletus. Rev. Youngun rocked, wondering where his seafaring brother was now. *Cletus wouldn't be a help. He's still an overgrown kid with a stutter. Law would split the kids up before Cletus even got home.*

Who would take them?

The church ladies had been coming around, trying to mother him, showing off their unmarried sisters, cousins, and friends, telling Rev. Youngun that he needed to get married again. Miss Bruster, Miss Louis, and the other single women were more bother than help in his mind. *They're just looking for a husband. Telling me that my kids need a mama.*

He thought of Sherry's recurring nightmares about him dying and her being dragged off to the orphanage. Ever since she and her brothers had snuck over to the orphanage, she'd had bad dreams about the place.

But who would take them if he did die? No matter how much he talked up the value of orphanages in church, he didn't want his three children to end up in one. *They'd be split up. Never raised as a family.* These were morbid thoughts, but in the middle of the night, when his worries were magnified, he couldn't help thinking the worst.

He smiled. *Maurice and Eulla Mae.* He thought of the Springers, their black neighbors who owned the farm next to them. *They love these kids and can't have any of their own. They'd take mine. Heck, the kids practically live over there anyway.*

Then he wondered what the law would say. *Can black folks raise white kids?* Missouri had strict race laws. *Got to check on that. Got to call the attorney and ask.*

Thunder clapped twice. There was a grist of rain coming. *There shouldn't even be laws about things like that. Laws can't make you love someone. The kids love the Springers. They don't care about color.*

Taking a deep breath, he fluttered his lips. *I'm not going to die. I'll get better.* His body was racked by another coughing spasm, leaving him unsure of anything. Sleep came between coughs.

6

Watching

❖

Henry Mead stretched the damp ache from his bones. He'd already covered five hard miles since daylight. Each step was agony. "Growin' old ain't no fun," he grumbled, wishing he'd slept in his bed instead of in the rocks.

The rain left the air wet and the glacier rocks slippery. Making his way back toward the watering hole, he looked for tracks, but all but the morning-fresh ones had been washed away. A raccoon watched him, holding a frog in its paws, then scurried away when the man got closer. Easing quietly over the great gnarled roots that had been scarred by years of rushing water when the creek wasn't dry, Mead worked to keep his balance. The rocks were slick-hot to his touch, but he kept on, looking for a sign that he was on the right path.

Columbine blossoms drooped on top of the leaves, giving some shade from the sun that was heating up the humidity which hung in the air like wet towels. Dried algae strips that hung like withered icicles showed quick signs of life, waiting for the rains to come again.

Slither. Mead knew the sound. *Slither.* He took two steps, then froze. His right foot hung in midair. Beneath him lay a coiled, banded two-inch-thick poisonous snake. Mead waited, counting the seconds with soundless clucks of his tongue. The snake rippled over the mud into the small pool, taking cover behind the rocks on the far edge.

By the watering hole, he found them again. Fresh monster tracks in the mud. Whatever it was, it had been here since the rain. The tracks looked like a man's handprints, with deep thumb and sole indentures. There were what seemed like knuckle prints, as if the creature was part man, part beast, walking hunched over. Mead had never gotten a clear look at the thing that had driven Rufus crazy, but now, seeing the long handprints, the claw points, he knew this thing wasn't normal for these parts. Taking a moment to catch a breath of courage, he surveyed the area, then followed the strange-looking tracks back into the bushes where he found a mound of wild fruit rinds and husks.

The stench of the beast still hung in the sun's glare. Whatever it was, it had passed this way, leaving its stink behind, floating on the humid air. The odor was a combination of rotten eggs, wet dog, and cat urine. It clung to Mead, going up his nose.

"Rufus, you here, boy?" Mead called out cautiously.

Boy, boy, boy, the ravine echoed back.

Shoulda heard that dog by now. Maybe he went back home.

Climbing on top of the smooth, jutting boulder, he searched for more tracks. The wind seemed to die out with only the hint of a breeze whispering through the pines on both sides. It took a few minutes before Mead picked up more prints, only these were different. They looked like those of a big cat. Maybe a mountain lion.

An eerie sensation came over him. The aroma of death hung in the air. Mead began thinking about the Mud Monster myth. *Was* this creature able to change shapes? *Maybe it's a demon,* he worried, looking around, believing in his heart that there were things that roamed the woods that were devil-sent.

He kicked a loose stone, debating whether he should go home. Then he saw something in a pile of wet bones, not ten feet ahead. Beyond the thick, shoe-pulling mud. Mead made his way along the jagged rocks that rimmed the muck. When he got to the pile of bones he stopped, wishing it wasn't there. But it was. Rufus's collar. It lay on top of the rotting, fly-covered carcass of what looked like a half eaten wild pig. A trail of blood led behind the rocks to another carcass. Mead looked at the thick, congealed blood. At the maggots crawling, digging, sucking on the bones.

The creature had eaten his dog.

"I'm sorry, Rufus," he said, squeezing the collar against his chest. He rubbed the dog's name that he'd burned into the leather, silently vowing to kill the creature that had done this. His breath came in nasal wheezes like a rusted screen door opening and closing over and over again.

Across the ridge birds took flight. He saw something race through the thick woods. He focused but couldn't see anything clearly. "I'll get you!" he screamed.

The thing roared back. Mead's imagination conjured up a creature, half cat, half beast, that flew on the wind of a stormy night.

"Gonna kill you," Mead said to the woods.

He could have, should have turned back. He was too old for this. Could hardly see worth a spit. But he was mad, and he set off to avenge the death of his dog.

The creature roared out over the hills again.

Sweat tracked down Mead's armpits. His mind raced like a weather vane spinning in the wind. His heart pounded in fear, throbbing in his ears. He picked up new tracks but they weren't the same. *I am trackin' a demon who can change shapes.* He began whispering the Twenty-third Psalm, vowing that from this point on, he would be a churchgoing man and bolt his windows shut every night. "Even though I walk through the . . ." But the words didn't come. It had been too long between Bible reads.

Then he heard the hooting call. Mead spun around, confused. The roar had seemed far away. Now the sound was somewhere nearby. No matter where he looked, he saw nothing but dark leaves, fluttering on the lifeless breeze. But something was watching him. He could tell.

In the tree above him, resting on the thick branch, the creature that Mead had been tracking watched him. Eating the last bit of fruit from the wild melon rind, he dropped it next to the remains of Rufus.

7

A Mansfield Saturday

❖

The wagon rolled slowly forward, the horses in no hurry to get to town. The wheels either crunched or rumbled, depending on the part of the road they were on. The horses clip-clopped over a yardstick-long black snake that had a tire mark across the center. Two crows fluttered up and down on the side of the road, waiting to feast. Maurice held the reins steady.

"Best kinda snake there is," he chuckled.

Dangit the dog followed behind them. Maurice was still mad at him for biting at his pant leg. Larry had his horse named Lightnin' tied to the back. Pa had said he could ride the ridge trail alone back home.

Maurice sang a ditty to Sherry, who sat squeezed between him and Eulla Mae. Her brothers lay in the back, watching the cotton candy clouds hold their positions overhead, waiting for the wind. They were on their way to town for Sherry to buy candy. Terry was scheming hard, but so far he hadn't come up with any foolproof plan to get it from her. But the more his sister blabbed to Maurice and Eulla Mae about the candy she was going to buy, the more he worked his brain for a way to take it from her.

The Springers had taken the kids along with them to be helpful to Rev. Youngun. They had been taking over food, doing the laundry, anything they could to help the man. That they were worried about whether he'd get better was an unspoken concern between them that they didn't let on to the Youngun children.

"You think Pa's gonna get better?" asked Sherry.

"Surely, girl, surely," Eulla Mae answered.

"What's wrong with him?"

"Doctor don't know for sure, but I think he's just got a touch of an early cold that don't want to shake loose," Maurice explained.

Two wagons passed by before Sherry spoke again. "You think he's gonna die?"

"Die? No, your pa's not gonna die," Maurice said gently.

Sherry closed her eyes. "Don't want to go to the orphanage."

Eulla Mae tried to hug away her fears and tell her not to worry, but to Sherry, they were only words in the air compared to the image of her father sick in the rocking chair. *Don't want Pa to die. Don't want the Dark Hats to come get me,* she worried.

Maurice turned and looked at the redhead, Terry. "Your daddy asked me to make sure you boys didn't cause no trouble in town."

"Why you just lookin' at me then?"

His brother, Larry, smirked, scratching his shaggy blond hair. "You know. 'Cause the 'T' in your name means trouble."

"I always get blamed. I'm just an angel," Terry complained.

Maurice shook his head from side to side. "God help heaven if you're an angel." He looked from boy to boy. "You remember what I'm sayin'. Don't nobody in Mansfield enjoy your shenanigans. I hear one peep, one woman screamin' 'bout a frog in her hair, see one girl runnin' 'round with a chopped off pigtail, and I'm gonna take you *right* home."

Terry put on his best shocked and indignant face. "You don't have to worry 'bout me. Think I'll just go to church and pray."

"Uh-huh, and I think I'll just lie down and die if you do that." Maurice turned back around and sang another song to Sherry.

Terry looked at Larry and shrugged. "Worse things been said about me." Larry didn't look up from the dime novel he was reading.

"How come Pa wants us to call it a bunny?" Terry asked after a moment, tugging at Larry's sleeve. The wagon hit a rut and bounced them around. Terry didn't like the new word that his father had told them to call the noise he'd made at the table. "Hey, are you deaf?" he exclaimed to Larry.

Larry put down his dime novel about King Arthur and the knights of the Round Table. "It's a bunny 'cause Pa don't want you callin' it the other thing." He didn't want to talk about bunnies. Larry was off in a world of good and evil, of battles in faraway places. Away from the worries about his father dying. In his mind he was a man's man. A knight of the Round Table. No one had noticed the changes coming over him. They only saw the baby fat that kept the cherub look to his face.

"How come it's always just me? You think I'm the only one who ever let a bunny?" Terry asked in disgust, sticking his hands in the pockets of his patched and faded Levi's.

Larry frowned. His eight-year-old brother was such a squirrel. "You're the one who did it at the table, blamin' it on poor Dangit like it was the dog who let the thing."

"Couldn't help it," Terry shrugged, sending a spit louie over the side of the wagon. "Guess you never let a tooty in your 'tire life neither."

"Not at the table."

Terry closed his eyes in frustration. "What's a kid to do? Turn blue in the face, blow up, and die?"

"Leave the table. That's what you shoulda done. You better not let another bunny at the table ever again."

"Don't think Easter's gonna ever be the same for me then," Terry pouted. "Can't imagine thinkin' 'bout ol' Peter Cottontail hoppin' down that bunny trail. Why can't we call it somethin' more like what it is?"

"Like what?" Larry asked wearily, ready to roll up his dime novel and call it quits.

"I don't know. Maybe somethin' like a fanny popper or privy wind. Or maybe buckshot or pants tornado. Heck, even tooty monster would be better than bunny. Bunnies are nice and cuddly. I ain't never heard of no one wantin' to cuddle up with the kind of bunny Pa's talkin' 'bout."

"I don't want to talk about it. Now, let me finish my story." Larry blinked, trying to get back into the battle scene. Knights were still all around, and he was riding up, carrying the biggest sword, ready to do battle for the damsel's hand.

Though they slept in the same room, played, shared secrets, and did everything together, the brothers were a picture in contrasts. Larry was tall, blond, broad-shouldered, and slow to anger. Terry was auburn-haired with tight muscles packed into a small body that never stopped wiggling. Larry loved to read, but books put Terry to sleep and weren't worth a bucket of warm spit to him. Larry could write stories, but a blank piece of paper scared the heck out of Terry, unless he was making paper airplanes. Larry was shy and reserved while Terry had spunk and didn't care what the world thought. Larry politely listened to and respected his elders. Terry was polite when it came to getting candy; otherwise he made up silly poems and did what he wanted, living for each unpredictable minute that seemed to spring forth without warning. When he set his mind on something, you might as well let Terry have his way because one way or another, he'd figure a way to get it. Like mismatched bookends, Larry and Terry hung together.

Now Terry was irritated. He hadn't gone to town to read a book. With his pa sick, the house had been like a tomb. He wanted to pull some stunts and connive a way to get some candy and have a jim-dandy day without his father knowing any better.

Maurice turned the corner where the Baptist Church nearly touched the road and followed the fingerboard sign to the town square. "Mansfield, next stop," he said cheerfully.

Terry sat up, excited. Though there was next to nothing to see in Mansfield, Terry thought that his little town was the center of the earth. He looked at the horses, dogs, and people milling around in the street ahead. He saw little kids peeking out from under the still-green hedges in front of the shotgun houses all oriented toward the road. All creation seemed to be up and about. On a good Saturday, with plenty of sunshine, two hundred people came to market to do their business. Half that number, counting dogs and cats, would show up in the rain. Terry knew it wasn't New York, but since he'd never been there, what did it matter?

"Where you want me to let you boys out at?" Maurice asked as they passed the bank and the dry goods store with drummers' wagons backed up, waiting to unload their goods.

"Don't matter," Larry said, eyeing the animals being marked for slaughter at the feed yard.

"Where you goin', Sherry?" Terry asked.

"Mr. and Mrs. Springer are takin' me to the candy store."

"Let me out there then," Terry said.

Maurice knew what Terry wanted. Candy. "You just be wantin' candy, so don't you be hangin' 'round the front all fired up and sad-eyed when she comes out."

"I won't."

"And don't be dawdlin' and pokin' 'round willy-nilly when you hear me call out your name. You come runnin' fast."

"We will."

"And don't be loadin' up on useless gewgaws."

"Don't need to worry 'bout that," Terry shrugged. "I don't got no money."

"Good. That way you won't be buyin' things you don't need."

"You want to loan me some money?" Terry asked.

Maurice tipped his hat to the ladies coming out of the linen store. "No sir, you ain't paid back the last loan you got from me. And 'sides, you just want to go get some candy, don'tcha?"

"No," Terry said, with a deadpan look, "I just wanted four cents to put in the church basket and a penny for cheese and crackers."

"You best be lookin' out for lightnin' to be strikin' you," Maurice responded.

Terry turned to look at Larry's horse walking behind the wagon. "Lightnin's still tied on the back."

"Ain't talkin' 'bout that kind of lightnin'. Now you boys don't go gettin' into any trouble. Your pa don't need no more burdens on his shoulders than what he's already got."

"Where you gonna be?" Terry asked.

"Eulla Mae is gettin' some supplies, and I'll be takin' Sherry here to the candy store. She's got a nickel burnin' a hole in her pocket. But don't you be gettin' no designs on schemin' some."

Terry put on his sad face. "Sherry, Pa said we should all share and share alike."

"Pa ain't here, and you ain't never shared none of your candy with me," she smirked, sticking out her tongue.

"You just mosey on along, Red, and keep yourself outta trouble," Maurice said firmly.

8

Shape Changer

❖

Mead picked up signs here and there, but it was hard tracking over the rocks. Whatever he was following seemed to change from humanlike hands one minute to cougar paws the next. The tracks confused the old man, whose mind was aflame with stories of haunts and boogeymen. It shamed him that he was afraid.

He'd grown up hunting game of all sizes in the woods—fox, bear, cougar, wild boar. There was nothing like the sounds of hounds baying up a tree. Mead's best memories were of waiting for rainy afternoons to interrupt his father's plowing so they could head off into the woods. Hunting was his life.

A sharp gust of wind blew suddenly through the ravine. Mead knew it was going to be a shy-moose winter. The forest seemed to be warning all its creatures of a hard, cold season to come. For the first time he realized how dark the woods could be, even with the sun high overhead. Every shadow made his heart jump. The monster could be anywhere.

The Ozarks could be as mysterious as a ghost story. Mead knew that one moment he could be in thick trees and the next in waist-high prairie grass or surrounded by rock.

Mead made his way through the bumpy ravine. The ravine walls were like the ribs of a skeleton. The outcropped bluffs and block streams were like arms and legs, pushing out through the meager soil that the plants and root-bound trees clung to. Mead looked around, knowing that the creature could be hiding anywhere.

The glaciers that had pushed down through Missouri lands had not smoothed it like the prairie. There was no rug of thick topsoil left behind. Mead was in the bare-bones remains of the left-behinds that the glacier didn't know what to do with. The land had a sense of brutality he'd never felt before. It seemed to be holding dark secrets that should never be revealed—Mud Monster secrets.

The hills were pocked with caves of all sizes. Mead knew that the creature could be in any one of them. He'd lost the tracks a half mile back, but he could still catch a whiff of the monster's stench. Sweat streaked his cheeks but he pressed on, determined. Across the small field he found the half eaten carcass of a calf. Pools of thick, congealed blood spotted the ground. *He's eatin' livestock. Next he'll be eatin' kids.* Revenge pushed him on. He wanted to get the creature that had taken his dog. But the land seemed to be turning malevolent—like it was siding against him.

The trail led back to the dark woods. Dark green algae trails outlined the rocks. The pungent odor of fungus and rotting leaves hiding somewhere in the cracks of the rocks assaulted his nose. Air squadrons of biting bugs surrounded him, but he still pushed on, calm and steady, determined to find the creature. A soft wind out of nowhere whistled in his ears.

The landscape changed again and again as he entered places he hadn't been since he was a child. The forest was wild, untouched. Honeysuckle hung from the branches, its sweet smell weak against the decaying stench of the marshy woods.

Once, up and over the boulder-strewn ridge, he saw the vultures circling. *Somethin's dead up ahead.* He stepped lightly, not wanting to make a sound. Kneeling by a half eaten fawn, Mead wondered if he should turn back, but he kept on. Each step was a step closer to this unknown thing he was tracking. The old Mud Monster rhyme came back to him from some misplaced file in his mind.

Monster, monster everywhere.
Who it eats, it don't care.

Stop thinkin' 'bout that. He frowned. He thought of the old Indian's tale. About the brave who traded his soul. *Can't be real. Can't.*

9

Sugar Prayers

❖

Maurice let the boys off in the middle of town, then parked alongside Bedal's General Store, which was a kind of all-on-one-stick combination store. "You bring your nickel on in here, and we'll see what kind of candy they got today," he said, taking Sherry's hand. He helped Eulla Mae off the wagon, and she went right into Bedal's to begin her shopping.

"Loan me a penny, pleeeeease," Terry pleaded. "I gotta have some candy. I gotta."

"Nope," Maurice said. "No use throwin' good pennies after bad."

"All I want is one red gumdrop."

"That's what I'm gonna get," Sherry smiled. "A whole nickel bag of 'em."

"You can have anythin' your little heart desires," Maurice nodded, helping her down from the wagon.

Terry jumped over the rail. "Did you listen to that?" he complained, kicking a cloud of dust. "'You can have anythin' your little heart desires.' Geesh! It ain't fair."

"It's her money," Maurice answered simply.

"But it ain't fair. We're family. She ought to share what she's got with me."

"Guess when you start sharin' with her, she'll start sharin' with you."

"I think she ought to lead the way. Show me that two wrongs don't make a right."

But Maurice and Sherry went toward the shop without another word.

The boys kicked around the streets, peeking into windows, waving to their friends. There was a group of men milling around the blacksmith shop, trading stories. A group of Indian women with baskets of apples walked to the general store to trade them for bread and molasses. Hogs grunted from the alley, their cut ears marking who owned them. They rooted for snakes and garbage, doing their best to keep the streets clean.

Terry didn't want to get too far away from the candy store, so he basically walked a circle, looking for a place to settle down and wait like a vulture until his sister came out with the goodies. He spotted Mr. Johnson, the nearly blind manager of the Mansfield Hotel. "Here comes Four Eyes."

Larry popped his brother on the arm. "Don't call him that."

"Why not? He's blind as a bat and wears glasses thick enough to ice skate on."

"'Cause it ain't nice. You know what Pa says."

"And Pa ain't here." Terry got down on his hands and knees.

"What you doin' now?" Larry asked.

"You'll see."

Mr. Johnson stopped and looked down at Terry, trying to focus. "Whatcha doin'?"

"I lost my new penny," Terry moaned. "I was on my way to church to put it in the poor box." Larry turned around, not wanting to be part of Terry's trick.

Mr. Johnson took the bait. "Why, here," he said, reaching into his pocket. "I'll give you one."

"Thanks," Terry said, holding it up. "You're all right, Mr. Johnson."

The man wasn't two steps away when Maurice came up and snatched the penny from Terry's hand. "You ought to be 'shamed of yourself."

"That's mine!"

"Nope, it's not. You owe me a penny anyway," he said, walking back toward the candy store.

Terry shrugged, sure that he'd think of another money-making scheme. The town banker, who held mortgages at six percent on most of the farmland in the county and considered himself a big bug around the Ozarks, made his way down the sidewalk. He was a barrel-shaped, older man with a huge, drooping walrus mustache, and mutton-chop sideburns. His face was a wrinkled mass of liver spots.

"Here comes Mr. High-Falutin' Walrus," Terry whispered, elbowing his brother.

Man does look like a walrus, Larry thought.

"Got a penny to spare, sir? I'm just as poor as Job's turkey," Terry asked, but the man didn't answer. "How 'bout a loan then?"

The man still wouldn't respond.

Terry was annoyed. "Then how 'bout con-tem-platin' the backside of a cow?"

Larry hushed him, but Terry knew that the old banker man had heard him.

"Man thinks he's the biggest toad in the puddle," he mumbled.

Two women from the church stopped and smiled. Terry wondered how they were able to pull their hair up into the French twists that were so popular. "You ladies got a penny to spare for the poor box?"

"You're the Youngun boy, aren't you?"

"Yes ma'am."

"Well, you can be sure that I'll put a new Liberty dime in the poor box and tell your daddy all about it. By the way, how's he gettin' along?"

Larry jumped in. "He's still a might sickly, but Lord willin', he'll be back to preachin' soon."

"He's in our prayers," she smiled, walking off.

Larry took hold of Terry's collar. "You better stop."

"All righty, I won't ask no more walruses or funny-haired ladies for money." He saw one of the Hardacre kids, a wiry, beanpole of a boy with a cornstalk cowlick that stuck up from his bowl-cut hair, selling chopped wood from his father's beat-up old wagon. "Wud! Wud! Wud!" the boy shouted, his crooked teeth sticking out every which way.

"Hey snaggletooth, would you lend me a penny?" Terry called out to the awkward, gawking boy.

"You better shadup or I'll come poke you a good one," the boy answered.

"Poke this and quit chewin' your cud," Terry grinned, wiggling off a finger doodle from the tip of his nose to pile on the insult.

Terry looked down the street toward Bedal's General Store. He could smell the sugar. Just the thought of all those wonderful, delicious gumdrops and hard candies made his knees weak.

"Lend me a penny for some candy," he begged Larry.

"No, you still owe me six cents."

"Then I'll owe you seven if you fork one over."

"No. I don't got one anyway."

Terry stomped his foot. "Cheapskate! You're so stingy I bet you'd skin a flea for its hide."

Larry paid him no mind.

"Bet you like to breathe 'cause the air's free!"

Guess I need to say me a candy prayer, Terry thought. He sat puzzled, trying to think of a good one.

Lord, I'll sing every church song and won't toss no spitballs next Sunday if 'n You'll just let a little candy drop from heaven into my mouth right now. That was the best prayer offer he'd made in a long time, and feeling positive, he closed his eyes and stuck out his tongue.

Larry looked at him. "What are you doin'? Tryin' to catch flies?"

"Just prayin'." Terry peeked toward the sky but didn't see any bags of goodies floating down. A fly buzzed dangerously close to his tongue so he slid it back in.

Lord, drop a gum ball in my mouth, and I'll help the next old lady with a mustache I see cross the street. He stuck out his tongue again but nothing happened.

Jutting his chin out, he looked up. *Lord, just give me a piece of Tootsie Roll, and I'll tell the truth for an entire day. Why, I'll even make my bed and won't sneak off to the privy when it's dish-washin' time.* Terry smiled. He was sure that the last prayer, the big one in his arsenal, would do the trick. But the only thing that dropped anywhere near him was a present from a pigeon sitting on the light pole above him.

"You think Sherry will share her candy?" he asked Larry, resigned to the fact that the Lord wasn't going to help him.

"She'll share some with me maybe, but not with you. You didn't share yours with her."

"But I only had twenty-two pieces. Can't hardly share twenty-two pieces when the doctor told me I needed twenty-two candies to keep my health up."

"You're fibbin'," Larry said, pushing his brother.

"Cross my heart and hope to die," Terry said, crossing his fingers and toes. "Honest, I'da shared some with her if I'd had more than twenty-two. But I gave you a piece, didn't I?"

"Half piece."

"Whole. I gave you a whole piece of my candy."

"Half. The other half was chewed on."

"Even with teeth marks it was still candy," Terry shrugged. "Least I wasn't tryin' to hand you ABC gum."

"You've tried that on me, but I was too smart."

Terry chuckled to himself, thinking about all the kids he'd sold already-been-chewed gum to. *I like to chew out all the sugar 'fore I sell it to 'em tellin' 'em that I'm just checkin' for poison.*

Six-year-old Sherry stepped out from Bedal's General Store in her starched dress, carrying a bag of candy, looking to Terry every bit a sugar angel from heaven.

"There she is!" He rubbed his hands back and forth, working the scheming section of his brain as fast as it would go. "I'm sayin' a candy prayer that she'll get the spirit of church and give me some."

"Good luck," Larry said.

"Luck ain't got nothin' to do with it. It's 'cause I pray a lot."

"If that's the reason," Larry said with a grin, "then you'll never get any."

"You'll see. My sugar prayers are gonna be answered soon." *Even if I have to grab her candy bag and run into the woods,* he thought.

Terry worked on his best smile, hoping he could trick Sherry without working up a sweat. If he got a mouthful of candy it was going to be a crackerjack day.

He looked to the left and saw the grim, dark-hatted couple whom all the children feared. "Bad news comin' down the street," he said.

It was the Robisons, the couple whom the kids had nicknamed "the Dark Hats," that all the kids hid from. They were the people who ran the orphanage—the ones that Sherry had nightmares about.

Larry looked up, hoping that Darleda Jackson, the pretty orphan girl, would be in the wagon with them.

10

Dark Place

❖

Pushing through thick trees that cut the overhead sunlight, Mead found the world a murky orange, a haze of uncertainty. *Monster, monster everywhere,* played again and again in his mind. The trail narrowed to not more than an arm's reach across. The woods rapidly thickened. Vines and spiderwebs reached out from both sides. The rutted dirt trail was littered with rusted items—broken buckets, pieces of track. He recognized the old mining camp trails. *Gotta watch my step 'round here.* A rabbit jumped across his path, startling him.

He didn't even see whatever leaped from the boulder to his right and knocked him down. All he heard was the loud roar. Then he felt the swipe of the claws and fell over the edge of the trail down into a black cave, tumbling to a bone-jarring fall. When he awakened a few minutes later, his shirt was ripped and he was alone in the dark, wondering if the monster was in the cave with him. His lip tasted salty from the trickle of blood at the corner of his mouth. His temples throbbed with fear.

Something moved. It wasn't far away. His heartbeat doubled. *Please, Lord, don't let me die in this dark place.* Sweat beaded over sweat as his shoulders stiffened in pain from the fall.

He dug in his pocket for a match and found one. When he lit it, he heard a hissing sound above him. He felt a trickle of sweat seep down into his britches. Somewhere up above him was the monster. It growled deeply. *Sounds like a cougar,* he worried. Claws scratched in the dark. *But it weren't no cougar that I saw sneakin' 'round my property. And them tracks with fingers weren't from no cougar,* he thought in confusion.

A deep rumbling from the pit of a beast's stomach seemed to shake the darkness. *Maybe it's a shape changer. A demon who can fly.*

The match went out, burning his fingers. Digging for another, he found a short wooden one and struck it against the wall. There, directly above him, two eyes glowed.

"Get back!" he shouted, dropping the match. He raised his rifle and fired, hoping to scare away whatever it was. The mind-numbing explosion left a ringing in his ears.

Alone in the dark, his eyes were burning, blinking rapidly for relief. His stomach gnawed with fear. Each breath was rough, making him cough.

"Smoke," he whispered. He looked down. The match he'd dropped had wormed into a brush hole and was smoldering. He watched the flame spring to life, moving through the darkness like lava. Near panic, he struck another match and saw that he'd fallen into an old mine shaft, filled with debris and dry leaves that were smoldering, eating up all the air.

The monster roared. Mead panicked. He couldn't climb up. That's where the monster was.

He took a last look around him before the match went out, and by the light of the flames, he followed the gravel path quickly toward where he thought the entrance would be. Crawling, coughing, and sneezing, bruising his knees on the sharp rocks and stones, Mead pressed forward in desperation. His pants caught on unseen nails. Goose bumps tattooed his spine. *The monster could be anywhere.* He tried not to breathe deeply, pulling his shirt over his mouth and nose to avoid inhaling the smoke. Then, seeing a pinprick of light ahead, he couldn't help taking deep, rasping breaths.

Mead barely made it outside. He fell down, gasping in deep swallows of the wonderful clean air, trying to blink the sooty, stinging tears from his eyes. He tried standing, but his feet couldn't hold the ground. It took him an hour before he could walk again and have enough energy to make it to town. By that time the mine fire had played itself out. He knew he had to warn the sheriff about the monster, so he headed out on wobbly legs and weak knees, with a headache so severe he thought he'd go crazy.

But he was alive, and Henry Mead was thankful for that. Still, he wasn't out of danger yet. The fear in the pit of his stomach cut and jabbed to remind him. The woods seemed unnaturally quiet. Not a cicada chirped. Mead was sure the creature was waiting, waiting for him somewhere up ahead.

Asylum Secrets

❖

Though the streets of Mansfield were alive with friendly, happy faces, Sarah Robison, who ran the Mansfield Orphanage with her husband, John, felt alone in her secret world of misery.

Old beyond her forty years, Sarah had a menacing air about her. The years had been unkind. Once pretty with golden hair, now worries and hurts were etched deeply in her face. Mental pain had been a constant companion in her life, a reminder of a past that never seemed to go away. Frown lines around her mouth and between her eyebrows were permanent creases of unhappiness, like a backwoods surgeon had done a job on her. The woman looked as if her whole being had been squeezed of good emotions, dried out, left tough and salted with misery.

Sarah and John had come into town for supplies. There were farm animals and orphans to be fed. They had more than enough responsibility for any normal couple, which they weren't.

Sarah's dark hat was pulled tight down over her ears as if she were trying to block out the world. The aspirin powders weren't working, and flashes of pain pounded her head. Her face masked the hurt she kept hidden in her clenched fists. No one knew that she had lost a daughter. No one knew that she had been confined to an asylum. Or that she and John had been fired from several orphanages around the state because of Sarah's cruelty to the children.

Choking down another powder packet, Sarah waited for it to dull the throbbing, pounding behind her temples. *Don't want to think 'bout losing my little girl. Don't want to.*

But the newspaper was full of stories about the children who had died of diphtheria, and that was how her child had died. It brought back the dark, painful thoughts she tried to keep hidden. She blamed herself for what had happened to Darley, her golden-haired daughter.

John, too, wore a dated black hat that covered his greasy, parted-down-the-middle hair. No one in town knew much about either of them, except that they had taken over the Mansfield Orphanage from the Wilsons.

Boom, boom, boom.

Sarah's head began throbbing, as if a surgeon were pounding her brain with a hammer. Nerves were fraying at the edges. The nail was being driven deeper. Inside her purse was the simple rag doll that could make her feel better. Her late daughter's doll. But she couldn't take it out now, in the middle of town. She'd never shown it to anyone. Even her husband didn't know she had kept it.

Boom, boom, boom.

The horror of the past was a silent shadow that followed her around. Memories of the asylum still haunted her. The cooped-up smells. The night screamers and babblers. Frantic, Sarah reached into her purse and took out the small envelope. The bitter aspirin powder was hard to swallow. The spit dried in her mouth.

Boom, boom, boom.

Can't let the Board know about my visions, she worried.

Her memories of the orphanages Sarah had been shunted between after her parents died were awful. It was a Death Valley of a childhood. She remembered being chased through the halls of the charity St. Louis orphanage by the cruel woman who ran it. Her life flashed by in painful memory blocks. *Made to stay all night in the trouble room. My toys taken away for jumping rope on Sunday.*

Then Sarah had met John Robison, another orphan boy, and had fallen in love. They'd run away, gotten married at fifteen, and had a baby the next year. Complications from the childbirth had left her unable to have any more children, but she had Darley. Beautiful Darley. For twelve years their daughter had been their whole world. When Darley fell ill with diphtheria, they didn't have any savings. It was cold and they couldn't buy any coal to heat their house. They'd lived on cornmeal mush, cornmeal cakes, corn dodgers, corn bread, and corn soup, which had slowly sapped their strength. When the money ran out, Sarah Robison had stood on the street and begged money for food and medicine.

Darley died clutching her rag doll. Just twelve years old. Sarah had fled in grief and was gone for days. The police found her walking the streets, mumbling, seeing things, clutching Darley's doll, falling down from dizzy spells. They took her to the St. Louis insane asylum where she spent a horrible year until her husband was able to get her released.

It wasn't hard to find small orphanages to run after that. When they first started running them as the live-in house couple, Sarah had sworn that she would treat the children differently than she'd been treated. That she would give them the love she never had. Only, each time she tried to reach out to hug a youngster, she felt a blackness come over her, as if she should punish each child for Darley's being taken away. John had tried to help her, and each time something happened Sarah would say the bad spells were over. But they ended up moving from orphanage to orphanage, hiding the past, hoping for a better future.

Things had seemed better in Mansfield until the diphtheria outbreak, which brought back all the bad memories again.

Dark Hats Comin'

❖

Terry scratched his ear, watching the creepy-looking couple riding toward them down Main Street. Their thick-bodied wagon horses clip-clopped, snorting loudly. The Robisons stared straight ahead, not waving, not smiling, looking for all the world like they'd never laughed once in their lives. Mr. Robison pulled the wagon to the public trough in front of the courthouse to let the horses drink.

"Imagine them bein' *your* orphan parents," Terry whispered.

"I feel sorry for them kids." Larry nodded. "They don't never get to come to town or nothin' anymore. No wonder the Dark Hats give Sherry nightmares."

"If I saw them Dark Hats ridin' up to our house, I'd sic Dangit on them, let loose Crab Apple the mule and maybe even tell Beezer the parrot to drop air bombs on their hats until they skee-daddled," Terry declared.

"I think I'd just hide and let Pa handle 'em," Larry said. *Pa.* At the mention of his name, they both fell silent.

"Think Pa's gonna die?" Terry asked.

"No," Larry said.

"You sure?"

"No."

The Dark Hats rode closer, neither of them acknowledging the friendly waves and tipping of the men's hats that was common on the streets of Mansfield.

"Just hope we never got to go live in that orphan home," Larry said.

"What if Pa died and we had to? Would you run away?" Terry wondered.

"Don't know."

"Would you dig a hole to China to escape?"

"Said I don't know."

Larry felt sorry for the orphan kids who never got to come to town anymore. He missed seeing Darleda, the new girl who'd arrived the year before. She was so cute that she'd taken Larry's breath away. When he first set eyes on her, he knew for certain that she was the prettiest thing he'd ever seen.

In his mind her face was carved ivory, her doe eyes precious stones, and her long, shimmering blonde hair strands of gold. The only things he'd ever thought pretty before in his life were Dangit the dog and the shiny dime that his seafaring uncle once gave him, but a girl? Larry had never even considered such a thing. Even though he told everyone who asked that he wasn't interested in girls, he had nosed around until he found out that her name was Darleda Jackson, and that she was from New York. Just thinking about her gave Larry the willy-shivers.

Larry wanted to see Darleda again, but he knew the penalty if his pa found out. Though he knew it was trespassing, he'd taken his brother and sister over the back ridge to spy on the orphanage. They had wiggled under the barbed wire, ignored the warning signs, and crawled up close enough to see everything. What they saw frightened them. The children were being yelled at, beaten, and humiliated.

The Younguns told their father about it, and he said he'd talk to the Robisons at church, which he did. They explained that when the children got out of hand, they had to be punished. Then, Mrs. Robison told Rev. Youngun to make sure his children didn't trespass again, and Larry had reluctantly promised to obey.

Terry and Larry had tried to put what they'd seen out of their minds, but Sherry couldn't. Ever since, she'd been having nightmares about the Dark Hats coming to get her. She had screaming fits about the Dark Hats dragging her to the orphanage, beating her brothers, locking her away. Her nightmares kept Larry and Terry awake, wondering what would happen to them if their father didn't get better. It was an unspoken worry that tormented each of them.

"Look at them Dark Hats. Why would anyone wear such ugly things?" Terry wondered aloud. "Hope Sherry doesn't see them."

13

Crazy

❖

John Robison pulled to a halt in front of the feed store but didn't get out. One of Mrs. Wilson's old "Adoption Day" posters had been placed in the window. He sat there, looking away, not meeting his wife's eyes. Adoption Day was coming up, and the Robisons had done nothing about it. Made no plans. They should have been out giving speeches, getting people thinking about taking in an orphan child, but a black cloud came over Sarah Robison when Mrs. Wilson's name came up. It was as if they were hoping that the town would forget the annual event where the orphans were placed with foster families.

Mrs. Robison believed the people of Mansfield were spying on her. Looking at her from the corners of their eyes. Whispering things behind her back—that she wasn't nice like Mrs. Wilson, that she didn't do as good a job with the children. That she was crazy.

A line of sweat beads formed above her eyebrows. Needles and pins pricked at her hairline. She wasn't ready for the annual Adoption Day when families came to see the children who had no parents. The churches made it a big deal, and Mrs. Wilson had turned it into an annual celebration. It was preceded by the meeting of the orphanage Board of which local ministers like Rev. Youngun were members, along with Dr. George. Mrs. Wilson was an honorary member and would be coming back from Springfield, where she had moved when her husband died.

"John," Sarah whispered to her husband, "tell everyone that Adoption Day's canceled. That we have our own way of placing orphans."

"We can't do that. We've waited too long. Don't worry. We'll make it through."

"But I can't get Darley out of my mind."

"Hush. Don't let it get to you."

Sacks of feed were tossed into the back of their wagon. The thick-necked stock boy covered them with a canvas and tied it down. Stephen Scales came out from the mail office and brought them a small bundle of mail. "Kids are gettin' a lot of letters from Mrs. Wilson, aren't they, Sarah?" he said, tipping his hat. Everyone still loved the woman who had founded and run the Mansfield Orphanage for forty years.

"Too many," Mrs. Robison griped, stuffing the mail into her purse. Her breath was sour. She didn't want to talk.

"What you think about all these letters?" Scales asked.

"I don't think about them," Mrs. Robison grumped.

"I dug out one of the posters I'd saved about the big day," he smiled, trying hard to be friendly to the unfriendly couple.

"That's nice," she said, not meaning it.

Scales looked at the bags and boxes of supplies that were already in the back. "Guess you're all gettin' ready for Adoption Day."

"Orphans are always ready," John Robison said.

"Think Mrs. Wilson will make it back?"

"No. She's too old to travel," Sarah whispered. "Let me sign for the feed." When she had written her signature, she turned to her husband. "Let's go, John." Scales just shrugged and went back into his office.

A farmer on a rattailed nag tipped his hat, but Sarah ignored him. Her greatest private fear was being taken back to the asylum. She knew there was something wrong—something terribly wrong in her mind. But there was no one to talk to about it. No one to tell about losing her beautiful Darley. Families hid away their mentally ill.

Maybe the spells are comin' every day now because of what I did. Maybe it's for losin' Darley. It was my fault, she worried, squeezing the rag doll inside her purse. The throbbing started up with a vengeance.

Her husband knew what was coming. Every time she gulped down the powder, he knew his wife was fighting back the meanness that seemed to live inside her. At the other orphanages she'd been able to hide it, but now the spells were coming every day. *If the Board finds out, they'll fire us,* he worried.

For a moment things seemed better, she could swallow. Then her mouth turned dry and the pain roared back in anger. Her nightmare memory fragments waited for the pinprick to bring them to life. Bits and pieces of bad events passed behind her eyes, like a disjointed nickelodeon movie show.

"You okay, Sarah?" John asked, knowing the real answer. The doctors had released her, saying she was cured, but she wasn't. Not even the faith healers had been able to do anything. Still, he clung to the hope that she would change; he hadn't given up the ghost of finding a cure. But in his heart he knew that his wife needed help. That she might be insane.

14

Edgar Allan Crow

❖

Larry looked toward Bedal's store, hoping his sister wouldn't come out until the Dark Hats had passed.

Terry saw the talking crow who lived in their barn circling overhead. "Edgar Allan Crow thinks it's a funeral," he said.

Larry said, "Hope he don't . . ." then stopped as the crow dive-bombed down, screeching, "Rise and shine!" Mrs. Robison swatted at the bird as the crow grabbed at her hat. Her husband dropped the reins, trying to help his screaming wife. The crow swooped over the horses, spooking them. In a blink of an eye, they bolted down the dusty street, scattering the Saturday shoppers. The orphans' mail flew out of the back of the wagon.

Sherry thanked Mr. Bedal for giving her the extra gumdrops. "Bet you gave me a whole extra half pound," she grinned.

"Close to a pound." The storekeeper winked.

Maurice slipped him a nickel. "That's for the extra."

"You don't have to do that," Mr. Bedal said.

"Then leave it as an account, 'case one of them Youngun kids comes back broke."

"You mean like Terry?" Mr. Bedal laughed.

Maurice nodded. "Kinda had him in mind. He's got a sweet tooth bigger'n you can imagine."

"Good-bye, Mr. Bedal," Sherry said, skipping out into the middle of the street. She stopped to take out a red gum ball.

Terry's eyes went wide when he saw his sister standing in the path of the Dark Hats' runaway wagon. "Move, Sherry!" he screamed and took off running to help her.

Sherry looked up and saw the wagon coming. "It's the Dark Hats," she whispered, feeling her heart jump.

"Get outta the way!" Larry shouted, but his sister stood frozen, like a deer caught in a hunter's jack lights. Larry ran toward the wagon and grabbed at the reins, hoping to stop it but was swept off his feet as his wrists tangled in the reins. A couple of men ran to help, but the horses were moving too fast, dragging Larry down the street.

Sherry stood petrified, her long, bony little-girl legs locked straight, the candy bag clutched in her hand. "Dark Hats!" she whispered.

Terry raced to save the sister he loved to torment, but the wagon was gaining on him. *Gotta save her,* he told himself over and over. Every second counted.

The Robisons bounced helplessly. The reins were out of John's reach. Sarah had fallen into the back of the wagon on top of the feed sacks. John shouted for the horses to stop, but they raced on, a galloping wagon of death dragging Larry down the street straight toward Sherry.

Maurice and Eulla Mae came out of Bedal's General Store. She grabbed his arm. "Maurice, look. Larry's caught in the reins."

"Oh, Lord," he whispered and dropped the groceries he was holding. "Don't let go!" he shouted to Larry, as he took off. He knew that if Larry dropped the reins, he'd be trampled by the team of horses.

Eulla Mae then saw Sherry and ran toward her. "Move, girl! Move outta the way!" she shouted.

"It's the Dark Hats," Sherry whispered, over and over, thinking her nightmares had come to take her to the orphanage.

Maurice cut directly in front of the approaching team, waving his jacket back and forth. "Whoa, stop there, ease up." It was a matter of great nerve because if the horses didn't stop, Maurice himself would be trampled. Eulla Mae closed her eyes. The horses didn't slow down.

"Stop, fools!" Maurice shouted.

Terry tackled Sherry, and they rolled into the muddy edge of the wooden sidewalk just as Maurice brought the wagon to a halt.

"You all right?" Terry whispered.

"Don't let the Dark Hats get me," Sherry pleaded.

"I won't."

"Is Pa dead?"

"No. You just had a fright. Now stand up 'fore you ruin your dress."
He looked at the bag of candy in her hand. "Here, let me carry that for
you. Too heavy for a girl to be foolin' with." Sherry was too shaken up
to think straight and handed him the bag.

Eulla Mae picked Sherry up. "Girl, you coulda gotten killed."

"It's the Dark Hats," Sherry said, snuggling against Eulla Mae's
shoulder.

Eulla Mae wiped the dust from the girl's face. Her dark chocolate
skin contrasted against Sherry's pale, ashen face. "God was with you
today," she said soothingly. A warm wind flapped the ruffles of her
blouse.

Maurice knelt down beside Larry. "You all right?" he asked, dusting
Larry's shirt off.

"Thought I was a goner."

"Your daddy's gonna be mad 'bout this," Maurice sighed, looking
at the long tear in the seams.

"Don't need to worry that poor man none," Eulla Mae said. "I'll sew
that up for you. Just thank the Lord you're alive. Praise God," she said
with fervor. Sherry snuggled deep into her arms.

"I don't know what in the sam hill started it all, but that was a brave
thing to do," Sheriff Peterson said loudly, pointing to Terry. "Saw it all
from down the street but couldn't do nothin'." He pushed the holstered
Navy Colt pistol back over on his side.

Terry came up smiling, his mouth stuffed with chewy gumdrops.
"Guessyou'dcallmeahero,huh?"

"What'd you say?"

"I'mahero,huh?" he mumbled, licking the sugar off his fingers.

"What's in your mouth?" Maurice asked. But before Terry could
answer, he continued, "I saw you racin' to save your sister. Bravest
thing I ever saw you do."

Terry swallowed the lump in his mouth. "Didn't want nothin' to
happen to her. Gotta love your sister the Lord says."

Sherry suddenly came to her senses. "Where's my candy?"

"Guess you were worried 'bout the bag of sweets too," Maurice
laughed.

"Who gots my candy?" Sherry asked, looking around.

"Did you drop it?" Eulla Mae asked.

Terry tossed the bag to his brother. "Larry's got it."

Sherry squirmed down and grabbed it. "He ate half my gumdrops!" she cried. Then she saw the Dark Hats get down from the wagon. She backed away, eyes wide. "That's the woman I had bad dreams about," she whispered, grabbing on to Eulla Mae's legs.

15

Out of Control

❖

John Robison was red-faced upset. His anger boiled over. "That crow attacked my wife!" he shouted, pointing to Edgar Allan who had flown to the top of the courthouse. The crow cawed back, daring them to do something.

"Crow don't like Dark Hats," Terry said.

Sarah made a move toward him, raising her hand. Larry stepped between them. "He didn't mean no harm in what he said." Larry dusted off his hat, putting on his polite face. "How's Darleda doin', Mrs. Robison?"

"The girl's getting along just fine, why?"

"Just wondering if maybe I could ride out and . . ."

"No visitors." Sarah looked at Sheriff Peterson. "What are you waiting for? Shoot that crow!"

A dangerous storm was erupting in her mind. Thoughts from the past were springing up like weeds. The face of the woman from the orphanage—the one where she grew up—was everywhere. She took a step forward and slipped on a half eaten sweet roll that someone had dropped, grabbing on to her husband's arm. Terry couldn't help but grin. The woman flexed her fingers back and forth and she tried to regain her balance. Sharp, pale fingernails slowly clawed the air like they wanted to bite into Terry's arm.

"You need some manners, young man," she said fiercely. In her mind she was back in the bad place. She wanted to stop, scream out, and hide, but she couldn't. All she could do was focus her anger on these children.

Terry stuck his tongue out. "Go claw a tree."

"Did you hear what he said?" Sarah asked the sheriff.

"Now don't go gettin' all fired up, Mrs. Robison. Crow just did what comes natural. Can't help it if your husband dropped the reins. And Terry—he's just a boy. He don't know no better."

Mrs. Robison picked her hat up from the dust where it had fallen and slapped it against her side, blinking back terrible thoughts.

"Sheriff, I think these children did something to provoke that bird." She glared, pointing her pain-twitching finger from Larry to Terry to Sherry. "They all look guilty to me. Someone needs to whip the truth out of them." Her intense eyes startled the sheriff.

"Easy now, Mrs. Robison. These kids might cut a few shines here and there, but no need makin' a great shake 'bout this."

"Shucks, only thing we did was try to help," Terry said, jutting his jaw out.

"You spooked my horses, didn't you, little boy?" she hissed wickedly, reaching out for his arm.

Terry knew from her tone that he was playing with something worse than a rattler. "They skeedaddled on their own."

Sarah grabbed at his sleeve.

"Don't touch me!" Terry yelled.

The sheriff wanted to say something but hesitated. He looked at Mrs. Robison through new eyes. All he could think to do was suck in his stomach and look big.

"These kids didn't do nothin'," Eulla Mae said flatly, putting her stout frame between the kids and the woman. Terry did a doodle finger on his nose from behind Eulla Mae.

Mrs. Robison was about to burst with anger. "I've seen 'em peeking at the orphan girls. Trying to bother the children," she snapped, licking the sweat beads from her lip. Her blood pulsed.

Eulla Mae shook her head. "They's just wonderin' why you won't let them dear little orphans come into town no more. Mrs. Wilson let her children come every Saturday and . . ."

"I don't want to hear about Mrs. Wilson. It's our orphanage now, and we'll run it as we see fit." Sarah closed one eye, looking directly at Terry. "Children need to be beaten to teach them manners." She felt the pain rising, driving her out of control.

Terry grinned, sticking his tongue out again, although he was careful to stay out of her reach this time. He was squirming, itching to make the woman mad, jumping around like a cat-chaser on the Fourth of July. Maurice squatted to pick up the scattered letters and handed them to Mrs. Robison. "Looks like Mrs. Wilson still loves her kids." He grinned. His smiled faded when she just glared.

"They're not *her* children any longer. You Youngun children, you keep away from our place."

"These kids just tried to save your life. Least thing you could do is thank 'em," Maurice said.

"I've heard about the preacher's kids," Mrs. Robison said, eyeing each child. "I've heard that they're wild, just one step away from the orphanage."

"And you're one step from the nuthouse," Terry whispered from behind Maurice.

"What did he say?" Mrs. Robison demanded, reaching around to grab at Terry, her face as red as a beet. Maurice blocked her.

Terry shrugged. "I said you got dirt on your blouse."

Maurice looked at the boy sharply, always amazed at the fibs that came so easily.

Mrs. Robison looked down, dusting off her blouse, her insides raw with pain. "I know what you really said," she whispered.

Terry knew in his mind that she was crazier than a one-legged dog trying to scratch for fleas.

"Let's get back in the wagon," Mr. Robison said, offering Sarah his hand. "You children do need discipline," he said as he gave the Younguns a stern look.

"Then discipline me!" Terry said, wiggling his backside, jumping up and down, throwing air punches.

"Boy, you calm down," the sheriff ordered.

"Our orphans may have nothing else, but at least they have manners," Mrs. Robison said.

Terry wiggled around, taunting her. "And dogs have wings."

"Enough of that," Maurice said, pulling Terry behind him.

"Spare the rod and spoil the child. That's a mistake we don't make. Let's go," Sarah said, taking her husband by the arm. They got back in the wagon and rode off without so much of a thanks to Larry and Maurice for what they'd done to stop the runaway wagon.

Sheriff Peterson looked at Terry. "Manners would do you some good. I learned mine in an orphanage. Made me what I am," he said, tipping his hat to Eulla Mae as he walked off.

"We all should say a prayer for them children out there," Eulla Mae said quietly. "Imagine them bein' your mama and papa."

"Couple of ol' warts, that's what they are," Terry shouted after them. "They were hatched from vulture eggs."

"Hope all those kids get adopted out. Somethin' wrong with that woman," Eulla Mae frowned.

"Wrong in the head," Terry agreed. "Think ol' Edgar Allan Crow grabbed all her scrambled brains when he pulled off that ugly hat."

"Terry, stop it," his brother said, but Terry was on a role, moving around, throwing air punches, shaking his shaggy auburn hair around.

"Matter of fact, I heard that she was born a wart on the end of a monster's toe, and he pulled her off and let her grow in the dark on a cow pie."

Maurice looked at Terry, wondering where he came up with such things. "Enough, boy, enough. Don't be gettin' yourself all possessed, like."

"And her mean ol' husband was birthed from a bullfrog, growed in bat goo and fed nothin' but snail slime till he was old 'nough to eat rusty nails." Terry would have kept going, but Maurice put his hand over Terry's mouth.

"Why'd you eat my candy, Larry?" Sherry whimpered, looking at the half empty bag. She threw it at her brother and buried her face against Maurice.

"That's what I asked him," Terry sighed. "I told him it was yours." He looked at Larry, shaking his head. "Shame you can't trust your own brother."

"I didn't eat any," Larry protested.

Terry tweaked his nose. "Gonna grow like Pinocchio's if you keep fibbin'."

"Come on, honey," Maurice said softly. "Let's you and me go on back to the store and get ourselves some more gumdrops. Think you got some candy credit there."

"Don't let the Dark Hats get me," Sherry whispered.

"I won't, honey. Eulla Mae and I will protect you."

Larry shoved his brother. "Why'd you fib like that?"

"It ain't right that I take the blame for everythin'."

"But you took her candy."

"I know it, but she don't need to know it. Now give me a gumdrop."

"No!" Larry snapped. He shoved the bag into his pocket.

"Share and share, that's what Pa says."

Disgusted, Larry jumped up onto his horse and rode off through the woods, following behind the Robisons from a safe distance. He had a hankering to see that girl again. The pretty one with the doe eyes. He had asked politely to see her and had been turned down rudely, so the "No Trespassing" signs posted around the orphanage didn't matter.

The sky hung as still as a painting overhead as the young boy rode off.

16

Through the Woods

❖

Henry Mead made his way through the woods back toward Mansfield. The rifle gave him small comfort. Rufus was dead. There wasn't anything he could do to bring him back. Henry's old legs moved fast. Something was watching.

I'm an ol' fool. Never shoulda tracked this monster. Shoulda left it to the sheriff, he thought, clutching the faithful dog's collar, a frown drawn tight across his face.

The stench of decomposition seemed all around him. The woods were alive, but the living things were hiding. Bird nests, squirrel dens, snake holes—all were empty. Like they had fled from whatever was in the woods.

Drenched with sweat, he could find no easy way back home for his old bones. Up and down the ravines, across the helter-skelter boulders, then back into the tangled brush. The open fields felt safe, but they were islands in the dark forest. Each step took him deeper into the overhanging darkness. The branches only allowed yellow-filtered daylight through.

Where he had once enjoyed the bleak splendor of the remote and lonely woods, it now chilled him, overwhelmed him with a sense of being isolated. He light-stepped, fearful for some reason that the ground would suddenly give way.

Man could die out here and never be found for a thousand years.

The tangled woods seemed terrible for the secrets they could hide. He crossed over a small creek, then plunged back into darkness. The stink smell rose again. The two-color leaves looked like creature's eyes. *How could somethin' so foul be alive?* he wondered.

Tracks seemed to be everywhere. *Can't tell what they all are.* He frowned, worried that he might be following behind the monster. Mead looked at the tracks of a big cat, his mind knowing it was a cougar, but worrying anyway that they were the monster's. A large raccoon, maybe thirty pounds and forty inches long stepped out ahead. Knowing that the raccoon was nocturnal, Mead wondered if something had spooked it. He came upon more tracks. Some were from the strange creature, and others were that of a large mountain lion. He looked at the manlike prints that ran off side by side—silent evidence that something not quite human was out there. Then they vanished as if the creature had jumped into the air, changing back to a mountain lion or whatever it became.

"Switchin' shapes again," he mumbled, wishing he'd never started the foolish hunt. *It was easier huntin' bear. This thing ain't natural.*

The creature was moving toward Mansfield. Toward the farms and school, where the kids played. *Gotta get to the sheriff. Gotta stop it from eatin' some kid.*

Mead was following the creature who had come around his property, but following him was something more dangerous.

It was a massive Missouri mountain lion. A big, snarling devil, mouth open wide showing its huge, sharp fangs. Its green eyes seemed to glow. The tawny, yellowish brown big cat weighed more than two hundred pounds. Slender in build with rounded ears and a head that seemed too small for its body, the mountain lion pawed at the ground with its small feet. Its toes, five in front and four in back, carried sharp retractable claws ready to extend out to rip open the throat of its prey.

It had survived by hunting the isolated Ozark woods, staying away from the towns and farms. But it was getting old and needed to go after slower game to survive. Like old men and children.

17

Sick with Worry

❖

ick, tick, tick.

Rev. Youngun watched the clock tick slowly, wondering where his children were. A hazy band of sun gold had crept across the room through the curtains, touching the lap shawl with the picture of Niagara Falls sewn into it. The curtains were supposed to screen out the details of the day, but the sunbeam moved with a life of its own, the light of God letting Rev. Youngun know that He was there. But the light didn't take the sickness from the minister's body. It just passed over him, lingering on his ash-brown, salted hair.

He was the kind of Methodist minister who wasn't too holy to lend a hand at a barn raising, sit up with the sick and lonely, or bring harmony to husbands and wives with problems. Rev. Youngun had hauled logs from the river, delivered babies, and buried more people than he cared to think about. He was a good man who didn't drink, cuss, or shirk his duty. His gifts of food, left on doorsteps without fanfare, had seen two families through the last winter. He did it all on little pay and a lot of love.

Now he was sick and worried about the future. He worried who would help him if things took a turn for the worse. He felt vulnerable, isolated, cut off from his healthy life.

Looking through the newspaper, he saw the obituary. It was a small one. Just a mention that Robert Parker had died from consumption. *I knew Parker. Ministered to his family. The man lost his appetite for living after he lost his livestock to barn fever and his mules got worms. And Leonard. That boy was the light of Parker's life. It nearly killed him when he ran off to Utah. . . . I don't have consumption. At least that's something to take comfort in.*

Dr. George had told Rev. Youngun that he'd get better. But the patent medicines he brought over hadn't done anything except make Rev. Youngun drowsy. *Can't be sitting here dozing off all day. I need to get my strength, my energy back.*

The call he made to the attorney that morning hadn't been comforting either. Worried about the lingering illness, Rev. Youngun had instructed that a will be drawn up. Not that he had possessions of any real value, but he was worried about who would raise his kids. The attorney had said to leave them to relatives, but there was only Rev. Youngun's seafaring brother Cletus, who was usually gone for a year or more at a time.

Rev. Youngun had asked Dr. George what he thought he should do. *He didn't even want to look me in the face. I wonder if he knows something that he's not telling me.*

The cough racked through his body. He'd lost weight. He could tell from the way his clothes pulled loose. *Who'll take the children if I die? Norma would want them to be together.*

If I'd have remarried, they'd have a stepmama. Only one woman had caught his heart since his wife died, but Carla Pobst had moved away.

Need to talk to the Stringers. I need to ask Eulla Mae and Maurice if they would raise my three. The attorney had said it was asking for trouble, to leave white kids to a black family, and Dr. George thought it would bring trouble out of the woods, but they were the two people Rev. Youngun knew truly loved his children. The fact that Eulla Mae was barren and had wanted children, was all the more reason. *They'd love the kids. With all their heart and soul.*

Sheriff Peterson had just called to tell him how Larry and Terry had rescued Sherry and the Robisons, and it made Rev. Youngun feel good to know that his children had been so brave.

Peterson said that the Robisons had treated the children badly, which upset Rev. Youngun. *I'm sorry, Lord, but I just don't like those people. I could never leave my children under their care.* Rev. Youngun looked up, wishing he could purge such thoughts from his mind, but he couldn't help it. *There are just some people you don't like. I can welcome them into the church, treat them in a Christian way, but it doesn't mean I have to like them as friends.*

Tick, tick, tick.

The clock struck on the hour, but no one approached. No one called. Nothing changed. His starched white shirt rode out from the waist of his pants, but he let it droop, unconcerned. All he could do was wait for his children to return from town and hope they weren't off swimming in Willow Creek.

He started to cry for no reason—and every reason he could think of. The sickness had weakened him and feeling sorry for himself was easy to do. Then he heard it. A faint, distant roar bounced echoes between the hills.

That sounded like a cougar. The animals in the barn answered back, frightened, making noises as if they wanted someone to protect them. It took a moment for Rev. Youngun to get up from the rocker. The lap shawl dropped to the floor, but he didn't have the energy to pick it up.

The animal in the hills roared again. "Need to get outside," Rev. Youngun mumbled, his voice thick from the medicine. The animals in the barn were in a ruckus. "Need to calm them down."

He heard the roar again and looked off toward the hills as he stepped onto the porch. The old boards creaked familiarly, but it had been weeks since he'd stepped out, so the wood groan caught his ear. It felt good to be outside, to see the sunlight dance on the pond. He heard Crab Apple the mule hee-haw. "I'm coming, Crab Apple." Crunching across the thick layer of fallen leaves, he made the barn rounds, then crossed over to the fence, where he rested.

It wasn't cold but he was chilled. *Can't overdo it. I need to take my time.* The cougar roared loudly, sounding closer. The unknown scared Rev. Youngun, always had, but he wasn't thinking clearly and began to make his way through the field. The woods weren't too far away, and he thought the fresh air would help clear his lungs.

He grinned, thinking about his mother telling him that curiosity killed the cat. His feet kicked up a flutter of dead leaves under the trees at the edge of the woods. Something hooted from the dark branches above.

Rev. Youngun slowly turned around, wondering what was up there. *That didn't sound like a cougar.* Then it hit him: the thick, pungent odor. Wind rustled through the trees, making the stench worse.

The strange hooting was louder. Rev. Youngun looked from tree to tree, trying to see where it came from. He took a deep breath, commanding himself to be calm, but his lungs quivered on the edge of a spasm. Within a minute his body was under control and his breathing back to normal.

The hooting started again. *Something's up there. I can feel it.* But he wasn't sure if he was the hunter or the hunted. For some reason, all he could think about were the Ozark tales of witches, hoodooing each other, fighting with their evil eyes. A shiver enveloped him. His body shuddered. *I'm too weak to be up here.*

A sweat line gleamed on his cheeks. His eyes seemed useless as the trees blended together. Leaning against a pine, he rested, looking around. Somewhere up above him something was making soft scraping noises, rustling the branches, scratching at the limbs. Rev. Youngun stood silently, hoping that his courage wouldn't break.

"Who-who," called out a big hoot owl.

"Just an owl." Rev. Youngun grinned, forcing back a cough. "That's a relief."

He turned back toward the house. A shuddering cough attacked him, leaving his body spent, wasted, winded. He coughed again, bent over, then hawked and spit, clearing his throat so he could breathe. It took a moment, but he managed to gather the strength to get back to the house.

Up in the trees, the unknown creature hooted softly, but the human didn't hear him.

Dime Novel Mission

❖

Larry rode through the woods toward the orphanage on a knight's errand, a young man at the doorway of manhood. Chitter-chattering birds called out, insects hummed and buzzed at the boy, but he hardly noticed.

Country life could shelter a boy from the sins of the city, but it couldn't stop the growing up changes that nature brought to each person. Somewhere between the waning months of childhood and the edge of puberty, Larry had felt things inside him that made him feel different. Made him see things through his own eyes and not those of his father's. He had no understanding that that was part of life's process. That he was growing up into the person he would be, shaped by the love of his father and late mother and the invisible hand of God he felt was always near him.

Larry Youngun was halfway through the gate of life and wasn't quite sure he wanted to go forward, to grow up and become a man. There was still the little boy in him who liked to play games in the woods, but the yearnings inside him made him feel different. Even his voice was changing.

Like the other young men, Larry had taken to riding the back roads, even taking the longer way to get places, because he wanted to do things his way. He had secret paths of his own, secret places and secret thoughts.

Though he still roughhoused with his friends at school, Larry had lately taken to being alone. To doing things without his brother. He had started spending what little money he earned on things he wanted, not on his brother and sister. Sure, he still shared, but there were things he wanted for himself, things he felt he needed—and needing to see the pretty girl at the orphanage again was number one on his mind. He couldn't get her hair out of his mind, and he worried that she'd be adopted before he could see her again.

A small weasel bolted in front of his horse. "Always lookin' for food," Larry said and laughed. A skunk appeared on top of a fallen tree, and Larry rode wide, not wanting any trouble.

He guided the horse through the back canyon, watching for slithering snakes. The descent along the rock shelf was difficult on horseback. He and Terry had no problem scurrying across the rocks when they played cowboys and Indians, but Lightnin' took his time. Larry remembered how the canyon dropped further still. Finding the cross point, he rode the horse across the steep, sloped ridge, staying clear of the sharp, jagged black rocks. The slope up the other side was slippery, so he kept to the line of small pines which clung to the dirt hidden in the rock crevasses. Something yellow-brown caught his eye—an animal probably—but it was gone in a blink before Larry could make out what it was. He figured it for a dog, maybe even a small deer.

Lightnin' snorted, smelling another, more dangerous animal that was watching from the woods. An animal that a boy on a dime novel mission couldn't protect himself from. It was the cougar.

It watched, wondering if it should attack the boy. It moved forward, claws ready, then stopped, seeing the herd of goats. There was easier game across the fields.

Blinded by Love

❖

The Robisons rode silently back toward the orphanage along the north road, through the hills, past the Hardacre section where the lumber men worked, and then across Willow Creek Bridge. When they passed the Younguns' house, nestled between the trees across the ridge, Mrs. Robison finally spoke.

"If we had those kids for a week, I could straighten them out. I could teach them some manners."

"Don't let them upset you," her husband counseled.

"They need discipline," she said through clenched teeth. "I'd teach each one just like the Sisters taught me."

"Calm down, Sarah. No sense bringin' on a bad spell when you don't need to."

That redhead should be whipped, she thought, gritting her teeth at the thought of Terry Youngun. *With a hairbrush. Every night for a month.*

John Robison watched his wife from the corner of his eye, carefully pulling his sweaty shirt away from his belly. He didn't want to talk to her, didn't want to chance setting off her terrible temper. *Hope the bad spell's not comin' on,* he worried.

He was also concerned about his wife's obsession with Darleda, one of the girls at the orphanage. She looked so much like Darley, the daughter they'd lost. Even their names sounded alike. *Sarah tries to mother her, hug her, telling her that we'll raise her. But Darleda always says her father's comin' back. That she's no orphan. That Sarah should leave her alone.*

Sarah's spells were terrible. When she lost control, the whole world was her enemy. In the first few years after she'd left the asylum, he had always been able to calm her down, but not anymore. She seemed to resent his efforts, as if she had given up hope of staying sane or staying out of the asylum.

In his mind he remembered the place she had been in. *The filth was horrible. Vermin everywhere. Crawling over everythin'. Disease killin' off the old and weak. Food not fit for eatin'. Can't let her go back to that. Can't. I love her too much.*

In his heart he knew that things were getting worse. That he'd been selfish, thinking only about himself and Sarah and not the children. Like a deep infection that sets into the body and wouldn't let go, he, too, had succumbed to her mean-spirited ways. *I've got to take control. Can't let her mind bend me out of shape.*

"You want me to do the plannin' for Adoption Day?" he asked.

"No. I think we should cancel it."

"We can't do that. Everyone's countin' on it."

"Countin' on what?" she snickered. "We've done nothin' except send out a letter. If we don't talk it up no one else will think about it."

They rode for a few minutes in silence, then John said, "The children need families."

"They need discipline. When they have that, someone will want them. But not before. Discipline is the key to love."

"You've been very hard on them. Don't you think you should ease up? At least until after the Board meeting?"

"I won't tolerate disrespect. I won't. I won't." She could feel the blackness coming on. The demon moods that fused the pains of the past with the present. She squeezed the doll in her purse, almost squeezing its head off. Her fingers pulled at the button nose, wanting to pop it off.

"I think we should both ease up on them. Feed them some treats. Get them playin' games. Children forget so quickly that if we make some improvements now, we won't have to worry about the Board members keeping us on another year."

"Why are you worried?"

"We just can't keep moving 'round like this."

"Movin's fine with me."

"Maybe this is the year you'll get well."

"I'm all right. Just have a bad headache now and then. That's all."

"No. There's got to be a doctor who can treat your brain."

Sarah slammed her fist down on the wagon bench. "No!" she screamed, closing her eyes, fighting back the intense pain.

He watched in silence, then put his hand on her shoulder, but she pushed it off. "If you don't want to talk to me about it, then let's go see the doctor in town. I love you, Sarah. I don't want to lose you."

But my love for her has blinded me, he thought, watching her grimace in pain. He felt the need to pray, to confess his failings. *I've tried to distance myself from what I knew was wrong by closin' my eyes. Tried to detach myself, escape, pretend I didn't know what she was doin' to those kids.*

The Board is gonna fire us unless we try to make the kids happy. Gotta get her calmed down long enough to get things ready for Adoption Day. Then I'll go see the town doctor and find her a cure.

Sarah hummed a nameless tune, reading over Mrs. Wilson's letters. Suddenly, in a fit of rage magnified by insanity, she ripped each one into shreds, remembering herself as the swollen-eyed young girl who never got any mail.

"I wish she'd stop writing," she muttered icily.

"Don't let it upset you. Her letters don't do any harm. Might be good to let the kids get them, with Adoption Day comin' up."

"No. Outside thoughts get them off track, takes away their discipline."

She read the letters from widowed mothers who'd given up their children. Twice removed relatives. They were about hard times, who was expecting, who had died. Reaching into the bottom of the mail sack, she found a letter from Darleda's father, saying he appreciated all the Robisons had done for his daughter. Asking that they put flowers on the grave every year on her birthday. Saying that he had left New York and was heading off to the Rocky Mountains.

Sarah hadn't told John about the letter and death notice she'd sent to Darleda's father, saying that the girl had died of diphtheria and was buried in the Mansfield cemetery. It was part of her plan to keep Darleda all to herself.

Each of Darleda's letters to her father related how bad things were at the orphanage, which drove Mrs. Robison to a frenzy. She burned each one by candlelight after she'd read them. So she came up with the scheme to tell Darleda's father that his daughter had died from the fever. It was the law that if the parent didn't come back within the year, that the child could be put up for adoption, which was part of Sarah's plan. She would adopt Darleda whether the girl liked it or not.

She read his letter again. *Good. Soon he'll be lost in the mountains and Darleda will be all alone. Just like I was.*

20

Unanswered Letters

❖

In Springfield, Missouri, Mrs. Wilson sat in a balding easy chair and wrote a birthday card to Little Jim, saying she hoped she could make it back to Mansfield for Adoption Day. Inside she had written: "And I know that this year will be the one that a family will take you into their hearts." Sending birthday cards was something she'd done for the past forty years for all the children she'd raised and placed out, but now she also sent them back to her orphans in Mansfield.

I wonder how they're doing? she thought, sealing the envelope. In her mind the girls were pumping on the Wilcox & Gibbs sewing machines, mending their dresses, singing hymns. She sipped her honeysuckle tea, taking out a mint leaf to bite. *Why haven't they written me back?*

She had taught them manners. Taught them to read and write. But, still, they were just children. *I know Little Jim will write back,* she smiled, giving the letter a kiss for good luck. "Orphans need love," she said.

The cicadas and birds outside the window reminded the woman of her years back in Mansfield. She thought of the sign she and her husband had hung over the front door: "Rainbows for All God's Children." The bric-a-brac covering the whatnot shelf on the sidewall were filled with mementos of her years running the orphanage.

The best years of Mrs. Wilson's life—almost her whole life—had been spent at the Mansfield Orphanage, which she and her husband had founded. Even when the air reeked of diapers that needed changing or when there was too much month between their money and the next church donation, it had been a good life.

Money was always tight. The children went barefoot to school until late in the fall, but she made sure they kept up with their studies. Every child got two baths a week and two changes of clothes, which they had to take care of. The kids worked hard. The girls darned socks and kept up the house. The boys toiled in the barn and in the fields. But at the end of every day, after the girls' hair had been put up into rag curls, Mrs. Wilson was there to give a daily hug to each one of them. "Never take a hug for granted," she'd whisper, tucking them in.

Her mission was to make sure that each of the children learned the difference between right and wrong, that they knew about the Lord and read the Good Book, no matter if they were Catholics or Baptists. She'd even had a Jewish boy for almost a year, and made sure that Rabbi Wechter, the circuit-riding, Hebrew-speaking man, came by to give the boy his Saturday lessons.

Every Thanksgiving she'd gone to each of the local churches, seeking donations for books and clothes, asking the congregations to reach into their hearts to see if they could take one of the children into their hearts and homes. Then, after receiving their love offerings, she read Scriptures. "He called a little child and had him stand among them. And he said: . . . 'And whoever welcomes a little child like this in my name welcomes me.' "

Her husband had gotten the cooperation of the town merchants to keep the orphanage painted and the children fed and clothed. Mr. Bedal, who ran the general store, had provided each child with an Easter outfit, and Stephen Scales, the telegraph operator and part-time barber, gave them each a monthly trim. Even if all the haircuts looked alike, she still appreciated his kindness.

There was no stigma for the children under her care; she made sure they felt part of the community and that the community in turn knew that it had a moral duty to adopt the children. It was the only way that kids could be placed into loving families, which was why they'd made such a big thing about the annual Adoption Day celebration.

When her husband died, Mrs. Wilson couldn't keep up the orphanage by herself. The place needed a younger couple to handle the work. So when the Robisons telegraphed, inquiring about work, she believed it was perfect timing. They assured the trusting, kindly old woman that they'd follow her example, give the kids plenty of hugs, and treat them like their own children. What Mrs. Wilson didn't know was that when she was packed and gone, the Robisons took down the rainbow sign that hung over the front door. Mrs. Robison burned it in a fit of rage. For the town of Mansfield it was as if the orphan children had dropped off the face of the earth.

In her mind Mrs. Wilson imagined that the children had finished their Saturday chores and were skipping double-Dutch jump ropes, playing ball, and running through the fields. *I bet the little girls are playing jacks in front of the living room fireplace.*

Even when she'd gotten too old to go ridge climbing, she'd managed to make every annual wild apple hunting trip. *Made sure each child got a pie of his or her own. Just like their mamas would have done if they'd been there.*

The Robisons had promised her that they'd write each week, giving her an update on the children. But she'd not received a single letter since she moved to her sister's house in Springfield. Not one letter. *I hope my children are okay. I hope they're eating three delicious meals a day.* In her mind she saw the neat and clean children, sitting four to a square table, hands folded in prayer on the starched white tablecloths which the hotel had donated, waiting for grace to be said.

She still couldn't get over the letter she'd received from Robert Jackson, Darleda's father, thanking her for caring for his daughter while she was under Mrs. Wilson's care. What had shocked the old woman was the part about Darleda dying from diphtheria. Her father was on his way from New York to Denver and was considering passing through Mansfield to visit his daughter's grave.

Mrs. Wilson had written the Robisons, asking about Darleda's death, but she'd gotten only a one-sentence reply:

Darleda Jackson died July 17, 1908, of diphtheria and is buried in the Mansfield cemetery.

I have to make it back to the Board meeting, she decided, wondering if she was still up to the journey by wagon. *First, I should call. Call and speak to Mrs. Robison, tell her I'm coming back after all. I'd like to visit Darleda's grave myself,* she decided, going to get her shawl. *Wish they'd sent me her last picture.*

There was a phone at the post office which she could use.

21

River Surprise

❖

Sniffing at his own stench, scratching with his knuckles and fingers, the creature rubbed up against the pine tree, trying to scratch the skunk juice off. But it was no use. The smell wouldn't come off.

Plucking a branch full of papaws, he fingered out the greenish-yellow fruit, picking, licking until he was full.

Listening to the easy wind, he heard the creek up ahead and bounded off, his long arms pushing ahead, knuckles to the ground. The green water was cool to his touch, so he lay down in the shallow part along the banks, soothing the bite marks from the dogs.

Taking a leaf that floated by, he crumpled it into a sponge by chewing it, then dipped it into the water. Holding it to his mouth, he drank, then filled it again. Looking at his reflection in the water, the creature hooted in sadness. He didn't notice the men in the flat-bottomed johnboat.

"What the heck is that!" shouted the burly fisherman, putting his whiskey bottle down. He rested a stubby paddle against the side of the boat.

His bald-headed partner looked over at him. "What you talkin' 'bout?" He tried to focus but his brain was besotted, unable to think quickly about anything except how sweat-sopping wet his back was.

"That! That thing layin' in the water over there," the fisherman shouted, his gesture rocking the boat.

The creature heard them talking and looked over at the pine-planked green boat. He waved and hooted loudly, wanting some food.

"Thing's tryin' to talk," the bald man said. They rowed closer. "Never seen nothin' like it." The burly man raised a paddle in a menacing way as they neared it. The creature took a rock and tossed it, then slapped the water with his hands.

"Watch out!" the burly man screamed, standing up. His mind and weight were off balance, and he fell over the side. He came up screaming, thinking the creature was coming for him. "Shoot it!" His partner took up his shotgun and fired wildly, capsizing the boat. They both splashed in the water, flopping around, screaming like there were gators in the river. The manlike beast crawled up onto the bank and ran into the woods.

Henry Mead heard the commotion and followed the sounds until he came to the creek bank. "What's goin' on?" he called.

The fishermen came out of the water screaming about what they'd seen. The drink had inflamed their imagination. The bald-headed man exclaimed, "We just saw a monster! Musta been twelve, fifteen foot tall, maybe seven hundred pounds."

"That's him," Mead said, looking at their red-rimmed eyes, smelling the aroma of bourbon.

"What was it?" the burly fisherman asked.

Mead hesitated, not wanting to be thought the fool. But then he spoke his mind. "I think it's the Mud Monster."

The burly man raised his eyes. "Mud Monster? I heard that thing eats but five times a year. Takes a person to its cave and feeds on the body. Sucks out your brains."

Mead nodded. "Things runnin' loose. Probably gonna kill some kids unless we shoot it."

"We? I ain't goin' after that thing."

His bald-headed partner agreed. "Me and Jake here never saw the likes of that thing. What *you* gonna do?" he asked Mead.

"Thing ate my dog and tried to kill me. I'm gonna go tell Sheriff Peterson 'bout it. Someone's got to kill this thing 'fore it eats some helpless kid."

The old mountain lion roared from the hill, scaring them all. "The devil-thing is part cat, part monster," Mead told them. "Switches shapes. Can fly too."

"No lie?"

"No lie. What I'm tellin' you is right as rain. It's the Mud Monster come to get us," Mead whispered, watching the trees. A deep-rooted sense of uneasiness came over the three men. It seemed like the woods were watching—watching and waiting.

22

Ten Feet Tall

❖

Doctor George tried to keep his 1904 two-cylinder Winton auto on the road, but the deep ruts in the road from the last rain pulled at the tires. It was hard driving over bad roads, especially while trying to eat from a sack of greasy fried chicken. "Daggone it," he moaned, seeing the grease drip onto his pants.

He wiped it off, then adjusted his glasses, hopelessly smudging them. The world was a greasy swirl. "Now look what I've done."

Rev. Youngun was on his mind. His friend was sick, but with what Dr. George didn't know. Nothing in his books explained what seemed to have a touch of catarrh and consumption to it. None of the medicines worked. What made it worse was his patient was talking about death. Asking Dr. George what he thought about the Springers raising his kids.

The man is talking like he's going to die. Like he's giving up. I worry when a patient starts talking about how to provide for his family when he's gone. He wanted my opinion about a black family raising his three white kids.

Dr. George shook his head. *Ozarks isn't the place to be talking about such things. There's a lot of hate still hiding in these woods that the Bible doesn't know about.*

I need to help that man get better. Well, I really need to help him want to get better. If he loses any more weight, he's not going to recover.

The toolbox jangled loose when he drove over the washboard section. It was a bone-jarring ride across the rocks, muddy holes, and fallen branches. The engine echoed off the hills: "Ka-HUNK, Ka-

HUNK, Ka-HUNK," like it was on its last legs, complaining about the five miles of bad road. But that was just the way the Winton cars sounded. Dr. George squinched his nose at the smell of the gas and oil drips burning off the engine.

Cars were a rare sight in the Ozarks and rarer still were mechanics who knew anything more than how to use a file, chisel, or sledgehammer to bend two parts back together. But with more than a half million cars on the road and America's favorite song being, "In My Merry Oldsmobile," it was just a matter of time until the big city ways came to Mansfield.

Dr. George finished the chicken, wiped his lips, then whistled a school-yard ditty. He didn't like driving with dirty glasses, but without hot, soapy water, no amount of rubbing seemed to take the grease off. It was stuck like thick glue.

There wasn't a soul to be seen. Even the Norskies with their washboard white houses that usually had a pack of kids running around stood silent. It was like all the Swedes had rushed out to the fields to work, leaving all signs of life standing idle along the road. He passed by an old hunting dog, one ear permanently folded down from a long-ago fight. The hound raised its good ear and dripped out a long, pink tongue as the car passed by, its engine straining to get back to town.

Shifting his thoughts away from Rev. Youngun, Dr. George began to sing loudly. He had just delivered his second baby of the week and was glad that God had blessed him when he took the job to become Mansfield's doctor. As the only black doctor in the Ozarks—and the only school-educated doctor for fifty miles in any direction—he at first had been somewhat of an oddity, but that had long given way to people's accepting him for his skill at saving lives and birthing babies.

Pushing up the sleeve of his stiff shirt, he lifted his bowler hat and wiped the sweat with his handkerchief. Then he put the hat back on, appreciating the thin band of shade it gave him. Still favoring doctor's fashions—with his long, black coat, gold watch chain, and St. Louis shoes—Dr. George wondered if he were the only man in the county besides the banker and undertaker who wore Sunday go-to-meeting clothes every day.

Thoughts of the undertaker caused Dr. George to worry again about Rev. Youngun's pale yellow pallor and the bones sticking through his cheeks. *Hope it isn't yellow fever but he doesn't have the signs. Wonder what's ailing him.*

Around the bend past the rumbling frogs in the marsh, the woods darkened, becoming so dense they blocked most of the light. He squished over a bullfrog in the road that had jumped in his path. To a man raised in the city, the woods looked dismal, dark, and foreboding. The deep bullfrog chorus faded out. Not a farm animal was to be seen. Dr. George gripped the steering wheel, his ebony knuckles whitening. It was always the part of the drive that gave him the creeps. He'd nicknamed it the boogeyman's road. A secret that he'd never told anyone was that he'd always been a little afraid of the dark. His parents had kept him on the straight and narrow, by warning him that the boogeyman would get him if he ever misbehaved.

I know there's no such thing as a boogeyman, he thought, licking his lips. *No such thing at all.* But the woods were dark. Too dark to see.

A bird called out, swooping down over the car and making him feel better. A red fox crossed the road. Dr. George figured it to be almost three feet long, not counting the tale. The reddish-orange fur, black ears, and bushy, white-tipped tail were unmistakable. "You'd better keep running or someone's liable to make you into a fancy hat," he called out.

Ducking to avoid a low-hanging branch, he didn't see the rock in the road, and the car was suddenly knocked rightward, out of control. The supposedly noncollapsible Munger pneumatic tire collapsed, jolting, shuddering the car until the rim ground into the soft shoulder off the road. The doctor groaned, knowing it would take an hour for him to change the tire by himself. Looking around, hoping to see a wagon or another car he could flag down to get help, he climbed out, disappointed that he wouldn't be able to make it back to town for a hot lunch at the hotel.

Working the busted tire off the rim, Dr. George noticed how quiet it was. The woods weren't speaking. Usually bullfrogs, birds, and crickets competed to see who could be the loudest, but all of a sudden, like the calm before a tornado, everything was silent.

"Must be a storm comin'," he mumbled, moving the tire back and forth with the crowbar. He tried to look around, but the world was still a chicken grease haze. Yet he could tell that the sky was bright. There wasn't a rain cloud to be seen anywhere. *So why are the woods so quiet?* It bothered him.

Dr. George hummed and whistled, wishing he had someone to help him get the spare tire on the rim. He wished he had his grandma's kerosene lamp. It was daytime, but he was still nervous. When he was younger, he'd huddled by that lamp to ward off the boogeyman. Now he was stuck in the dark woods. *I need to hurry up. I need to get back to town.*

Then he smelled it. Drifting down from the tree line came the stink. Worse than spoiled chicken. Adjusting his glasses, he looked around and saw two crows circling. *Just something dead. Nothing to worry about.* Gripping the crowbar tightly, he turned slowly around, ready for whatever was coming.

"I might be getting worried for no reason," he whispered. "Probably just a dead animal." But it smelled worse than a decaying rat trapped in the walls. And he couldn't see it because his vision was still chicken-grease cloudy.

Working as fast as he could, sweat dripping from his forehead and ears, he got the spare tire on the rim and coughed loudly, trying to scare away whatever was out there. His heart was beating hard. "I'm going to make it back to the hotel for lunch. I'll order a double helping of whatever they're serving." Truth was he was scared. He could hardly breathe and thought he might just up and croak right there on the side of the road.

Then he heard the dragging, shuffling sound coming toward him, like someone was coming through the woods. He looked around but couldn't see anything clearly. Sweat dripped from his forehead, making the glasses worse.

"Lord, what's coming?" he whispered, looking around. His legs felt like rubber as the sound came closer and closer. Dr. George thought about running off. *Thing can probably move faster than lightning. I can get in the car and take off—start the engine and take off.* But he didn't move. It was as if he were rooted out of fear and morbid curiosity. It took a moment to realize that the pounding, booming noise in his ears was his own heartbeat.

"I can't see a thing!" he snapped, sticking the glasses into his breast pocket.

His eyes wide, on the edge of panic, Dr. George finally saw something standing, half hidden by the bushes about fifty feet away. It was big, tall, hairy, and ugly. He squinted, trying to see it better, but his eyesight was poor without his glasses. One second the creature seemed ten feet tall, the next it was fifteen. Dr. George backed away, climbing up onto his open air car, his face tight with fear, wishing he had covers to pull over his head.

"Now you just go on back. I don't mean you no harm," he said, unsure whether it was a man or beast he was looking at. The creature didn't move.

He rubbed his eyes. "I said leave me alone." Slowly reaching for the switch, he started the car.

"Hoot, hoot, hoot!" the creature screamed.

The creature ran forward on his feet and arms, hooting loudly. In the doctor's terrified mind it was evil come to life. He called out for the Lord to protect him like he was calling a lost friend in the dark.

"Go on! Stay back!" Dr. George shouted, fumbling with the choke. He'd have jumped into a hole if he could have pulled something over him to hide under. Finally getting the car into gear, he chugged down the hill wishing that his horseless carriage had a team of horses pulling it. The creature grabbed at the back wheels and scratched at the door. Dr. George tried to turn around, but the creature jumped up onto the car, wrapping his arms around Dr. George's face.

"Get off! Get off!" Dr. George shouted, pushing back the filthy, stinking thing, seeing his life pass before his eyes.

The creature's wet tongue licked his ears. Dr. George was sure he was about to die. "Get off me!" He hit a deep rut and the creature bounced off, rolling into the dirt. The last thing Dr. George saw as he rounded the bend was the creature running back into the woods. He kept the gas pedal floored.

23

Just Another Orphan

❖

Darleda had no idea that Mrs. Robison had sent her father a death notice. Cut off from the world, not allowed to visit the town or talk with anyone but the other orphans, Darleda could only hope that her father would answer her letters. *At least Mrs. Robison isn't trying to mother me anymore. That was awful.* There was something about the woman that bothered Darleda. Something that didn't seem right. The girl found it hard to understand how Mrs. Robison could have gone from smothering her to tormenting her.

I wish Father would come back. He should have been here by now. Fighting off the feelings of abandonment, guilt, and hopelessness was a daily battle. The stark, structured, lonely existence, in an atmosphere of terror, where a leather strap was always present, made life miserable. She felt lower than dirt.

Adoption Day was on her mind. If her father didn't write back or return by that time, she could be legally adopted. It had been over a year since he had left, so the law said she could now be placed with another family. All the other kids were excited, hoping they'd be taken in by nice families, but Darleda had vowed to run away to New York and find her father.

There was something about Darleda that just caught your eye. Almost a glow. Her face was somewhere between a girl and a woman. She was supposed to be doing her chores, would be punished if she didn't, but every time the Robisons left, the pretty girl did simple things, like writing letters and working on her poetry, things she wasn't allowed to do during the day when the Robisons were around.

The other children were cleaning, darning, making bread, washing the steps, chopping wood, making soap from ash and grease drippings, pickling cucumbers, churning butter—it was a never-ending list of chores that lasted from light to dark.

Blowing the ink dry, Darleda quickly read the letter again, then added, *please write back.* It had become a weekly ritual of hope, a lifeline to her past and future. Even though Mrs. Robison said she took the letters to town each week to mail, Darleda suspected that her letters weren't getting through—that Mrs. Robison was destroying them. Yet each letter gave more detail of the terrible things going on at the orphanage. *When Daddy gets back, he'll straighten things out.*

Darleda put the letter in the mail basket in the front room. All she could do was hope that this one would get through to her father. *Maybe something's happened to Daddy. Maybe he died like Mother. Maybe that's why he's not written back.*

She didn't want to think about her mother's death during childbirth. Dying by the side of the road. Her father blaming himself for not being able to deliver their baby and save his wife. Both had died. He had grieved deeply, saying over and over that God must have been angry with him. That He took his wife and baby as punishment. Darleda worried that he'd go crazy. It went on like that for three days after the burial.

He decided that they should first go back to New York to get his old mother whom they'd planned to send for later when they'd homesteaded a place. She would be able to help raise Darleda while he found work. With the money running low, they could only afford to buy a wagon and set out on the long, hard way, but the wagon had repeatedly broken down and they'd ended up in Mansfield, nearly broke.

In a panic, her father had gone to the Mansfield Orphanage and talked with the kindly old couple who ran the place. Mrs. Wilson had taken her father's hand and stood under the sign. "You see those words, *Rainbows for All God's Children*? That's how we raise all our children here. With God's love."

"That's what my little girl needs. A woman's kindness. Losin' her mother's 'bout killed her."

"We'll take good care of her. You just hurry and come back," Mrs. Wilson said.

Darleda could hear her father's last words as if they were still hanging in the air. "I'll only be gone a few months. You'll be in good hands with the Wilsons."

"Take me with you, Daddy," she had pleaded. "I'll be good. I won't get in the way."

"I can't. I need to work my way back to New York so I can have the money to come back."

"Please don't leave me."

Mrs. Wilson had hugged her. "You'll be all right. Just a few months till your pa comes back. It'll give you a chance to play with the other children."

"Trust me. I'll come back," her father repeated. "You're the sun and moon of my life. Without you and your golden hair, there'd be no sun over my Rocky Mountains." He left her with Mrs. Wilson, saying, "Take care of my little rainbow. I'll be back."

Then he was gone. Darleda worried that she'd never see him again. For the first few weeks, life had been bearable. The other children were nice to her and the Wilsons did their best to love her. The old couple knew the pain of orphans since they'd both been abandoned when they were young. Some nights, after lights out, Mrs. Wilson would find Darleda staring out the window.

"Your daddy will come back. Don't you worry."

"But when?"

"When he gets here. He loves you. Don't you ever forget that."

"But I wish I could see him now. Wish I could know he was on his way."

The old woman had wrapped her arms around the girl, then went over to the dresser. She brought back a candle and struck a wooden match. She handed the flickering candle to Darleda saying quietly, "A man once told me that it's better to light a candle than to curse the darkness. I think he was right." Darleda had sat up that night until the candle had burned itself out, sending prayers on shooting stars that her father would be back soon.

Now more than a year later, she had no idea that her father was nearing the Missouri line on his way to Denver aboard the Union Pacific rail line. There was no question that he was going to finish the trip that had brought so much misery into his life. The only decision to be made was whether he would visit Darleda's grave in Mansfield.

Robert Jackson's life the past year hadn't been good. Tragedy after tragedy. A hard luck chain of bad road. His wife and baby had died, he'd had to leave his daughter in an orphanage, and when he got to New York, his mother was dead.

Denver's gonna be better. Gonna be a fresh start, he thought, ducking the cinder that flew back from the train engine. Memories of the family he'd once had, of his wife, of the last time he saw Darleda flooded back over him. Since leaving Darleda at the orphanage, he'd lost twenty pounds. His Levi's hung loose, with room to spare.

He remembered how she used to shriek when he tossed her in the air when she was little. *Used to tell her that I'd always be there for her. Then I left her in that home where she caught sick and died.*

He recognized the bend in the river under the trestle. Where the trees hung low, full of small, wispy leaves, like green mist. *Crossed here before. When I had the family with me. When Caroline was big with the baby comin'.*

The doctor had thought his wife was just six months along. He said they could travel west by train and she'd deliver in Denver. Where the snowcapped mountains were. The city of their dreams that they'd read so much about. But the doctor had misjudged her time. Probably because she hadn't gained much weight during the pregnancy. Her due date was close, the baby wouldn't wait. Her time came when the train broke down near Springfield. The conductor got them a wagon from a nearby farm and sent them to find a doctor.

His wife had gone into labor on the side of the road. Next to a battered mailbox that was leaning sideways, too tired for mail. *Caroline moaning. Darleda crying. I'd never delivered a baby before. Didn't know what to do.* He'd done his best to bring the baby into the world.

Wasn't nothing I could do to save Caroline or the baby.

He wiped the tears with his sleeve. *Now Darleda's buried in Mansfield. No kin helped lower her down. Ain't right. This might be my only chance to pay my last respects.*

If he could rent a horse at the stop near Mansfield, he'd ride hard to see the grave and make it back before the train headed on to Denver.

24

Candy Madness

❖

The creature watched, looking through the branches. He saw a wagon with a man and two children. The creature stared, examining their faces and clothes, wondering if these humans would try to kill him. His stomach growled. Food. That's all the creature could think about: getting more to eat. Making his way carefully down the hill, the creature determined to get to the wagon.

Terry was talking up a storm, asking Maurice every question he could think of, while his mind schemed to get to the front of the wagon where the candy was. The languid fall heat was making him nervous; like a cat near milk, he needed candy. He wanted to put Maurice off guard so he could figure a way to swipe Sherry's candy bag. The problem was that she'd been holding the bag so tightly that Terry had begun to worry that it was hopeless. His stomach felt like a bagful of squirming eels. *There has to be a way,* he thought, his eyes filled with sweet hope.

Dangit lay on the food sacks, smelling the salt-wrapped bacon, his long pink tongue drooling with each sniff. "Mr. Springer, why do dogs have wet noses?" Terry asked.

"'Cause they don't have handkerchiefs. What kind of question is that?"

"Just wonderin'," Terry said, eyeing the piece of candy heading for Sherry's lips. He inched closer. "Well then, why do worms come out after it rains?"

"They don't wanna drown. Don't you know that?"

"No, that's why I was askin'. 'Cause you're so smart."

Maurice took the bait and grinned. "Ask me another."

"Can't hear you," Terry said, inching up from the back of the wagon, his eyes locked on the bag. He said another sugar prayer, and lo and behold, Sherry set the bag down on the seat. Terry grinned, winking up at the sky.

"Test me again." Maurice beamed.

"Okay then, why can't we tickle ourselves?"

"That's easy. 'Cause it ain't no fun."

"Look over there!" Terry shouted, pointing to the right. Sherry turned quickly. Terry had his hand halfway into the bag when she caught him.

"You're tryin' to thief my candy," she shouted.

"Was not! The bag was fallin' so I grabbed it."

"I'll bet," she smirked, sticking her tongue out and clutching the bag.

"Seems I should at least get a reward for keepin' it from fallin' over." Maurice shrugged. "Ask me a question about farm animals that I can't answer, and I'll give you piece of pie when we get back."

Terry scratched his chin, thinking of a good one. "Okay then," he said, "which came first, the chicken or the egg?"

"That's easy, the egg."

"But where'd the egg come from?"

"Well, the chicken."

"So which came first?" Terry smiled, wanting to laugh.

Maurice cleared his throat. "No more of these *stupid* questions. The answer is the egg first, then the chicken, and then you just hush up. I'm tired of you askin' so many fool questions."

The creature stopped. He had gotten ahead of the wagon. Cocking his head, he wondered about them. They were talking. Making noise. Just like before. Just like the other ones. Moving slowly through the bushes the creature wondered if he should just run up and jump into the wagon. Where the small human was in the back.

Maurice halfheartedly flicked the whip-strike in the air above the flanks of the chestnut-colored horses. He was in no hurry, enjoying the silly talk from the two Younguns. Eulla Mae couldn't have kids, which he'd accepted as the Lord's will, so he made the best of times he spent with the Younguns. He rode along, joshing with them, letting the horses pull slowly along the side road back home. All he could think about was the sweet potato pie that Eulla Mae would have ready for him at home. She'd ridden home earlier in cousin Thelma Lou's new buggy so she could get supper ready.

Maurice began singing made-up words to his favorite song:

"Swing low, sweet potato pie
Maurice is comin' to get him some,
Gonna eat five pieces in a blink of an eye,
Then I'm gonna have another one."

"No sir, there's nothin' as good as a Eulla Mae Springer sweet potato pie." He started singing again.

Terry covered his ears in the back of the wagon. He had a headache. A candy headache. It was the worst feeling of all. Terry knew that if he didn't figure a way to get that candy bag from Sherry, he'd probably shrivel up and die faster than a snail being shook in a bag full of salt.

"What's wrong with you?" Maurice asked, looking back from the front of the wagon.

"I'm sick."

"Sick? What's wrong, boy?"

"Think I'm havin' a spell of somethin'," Terry moaned.

"Uh-huh. And if you could spell it, I'd believe it. Me, why, I think you be thinkin' 'bout somethin' you shouldn't be thinkin' 'bout that's not yours." He looked at the boy. "Redhead, you're wearin' your wants like a red scarf at a funeral."

"What's that? What's he want?" Sherry asked, turning around, showing a mouthful of candy. She knew good and well what Terry wanted.

Terry pretended to be upset. "And that's the thanks I get for savin' your worthless life. Shoulda let that wagon of warts runned over you, squish you flat as a stink bug."

"I *said* thank you."

"And here I am, sufferin' from the worst thing in the world."

"And what's that?" Sherry wondered, poking through the bag of candy until she found a red gumdrop.

"I'm havin' a C-M spell."

Maurice raised his eyebrows. "C-M? What's that?"

"Candy madness," Terry moaned, rubbing his head. "If I don't get a piece of candy to eat, my teeth are gonna fall out, my ears will melt, and my nose will fly up in the air and land in your mouth," he said, looking directly at his sister. "And it'll have a sneeze built up in it so when it hits your lips it'll explode like a nose bomb."

"Will not," she said, eating another gumdrop.

Terry knew the bag was getting lighter in her hands. It *looked* lighter. It smelled lighter. There was just a little sugar left in there, and he had to have it. "Good-bye, Mr. Springer," he whispered, rolling around in the back of the wagon. "I'm dyin'. Goin' up to heaven on the wings of angels." Dangit the dog cocked his head, wondering what the crazy boy was up to now.

"See you later," Maurice nodded, like it was no big deal. "Say hello to Saint Peter for me."

"And I can feel my teeth fallin' out," Terry moaned, slyly taking some corn kernels from the hole in the feed sack and sticking them into his mouth.

Sherry turned, curious now to see what he'd do next. "You still gots your teeth," she said.

"No, they're fallin' out," he coughed, spitting the corn kernels all over her. Sherry screamed, trying to wipe the mess off her face. Terry reached into the newspaper-wrapped bacon that Maurice and Eulla Mae had bought at Bedal's store and pulled off a hunk of fat. "And here's my nose," he shouted, hitting her right between the eyes with the white, greasy mess.

"Get his nose off me!" Sherry screamed. Terry faked a sneeze in her face.

Dangit smelled the bacon and began howling. Maurice pulled at the bacon mess on her forehead and tossed it to the dog. Terry took advantage of the mayhem and snatched the candy bag, rolled backward and emptied the sweet sack of gumdrops into his mouth, then placed the empty bag in front of Dangit who promptly stuck his nose inside to lick at the sugar.

Maurice pulled the wagon off to the side of the road until things had calmed down. Sherry was fit to be tied. "Terry gots my candy! He gots my candy!"

"Think Dangit got it, girl," Maurice said.

"Terry ate it, I know he did," she cried.

Maurice gave Terry the eye. "Did you eat the bag?"

Terry wasn't lying. He hadn't eaten the actual bag. He'd just eaten all the rest of the candy. "No sir, but Dangit, he sure tried." Dangit cocked his head, his nose hidden by the candy bag which was still over his snout. Terry savored the sweet residue of candy which he kept burping up, over and over, wishing his tongue was long enough to lick inside his tummy.

"Gonna make sure you sniff some vanilla to calm you down when I get you home. In all my born days I ain't never run across a body such as you." Maurice sighed.

"I'll eat some vanilla gumdrops with my nose if you got any," Terry offered, turning around just long enough to lick the last residue of sugar from his fingers.

"Mr. Springer, why do you let him get 'way with everythin'?" Sherry asked.

Maurice looked at the pretty girl and shrugged. "Just that whenever I go to thinkin' that I shouldn't be puttin' up with his stuff, why, I get to thinkin' how much God's put up with me. Guess it kind of balances things out, don't it?"

"But he's a rotten apple."

Maurice looked Terry in the eye as he answered. "You sometimes find a worm even in a good apple."

"Where's the apple?" Sherry asked. "I only see a worm."

Terry needed to change the subject. "What if you lost your balance while you were walkin' a tightrope, what would you do?"

"Wouldn't be walkin' on no tightrope," Maurice snapped, knowing that Terry was up to something.

"And what if your underpants froze up in the dead of winter and you had to go?"

"Quit askin' them fool questions. Sometimes I think that under all that auburn hair, there's nothin' in that thick skull of yours but nitwits." Then Maurice sniffed the air. "You kids smell somethin'?"

"Sherry let a bunny," Terry taunted.

"Hush," Maurice whispered, looking around. He reached under the wagon seat and pulled out his shotgun.

"What's wrong?" Sherry whimpered, wrapping herself around his waist.

"Move off, child, I got to have me a look 'round," Maurice said, pulling the wagon to a halt.

"For what?" Terry asked, his eyes as big as silver dollars.

Then the children too noticed the terrible stench. It was coming from the bushes not fifteen feet away. Maurice was the first to see the big eyes and yellow teeth set in the hairless, dark face. The horses began to spook. "Sweet Jesus protect me," he muttered, holding the reins tight.

Maurice raised the shotgun. "Whatever you is, be gone. Don't be hauntin' us."

The eyes just stared, boring into them. The deathly silence was smothered by the horrible stench. Maurice pulled back the hammer. "Stay away. We're just passin' by."

"You better get gone!" Terry shouted. He took a handful of corn kernels and threw it at the bushes. The creature blinked and fell back. They could hear stamping feet and a strange hooting. Maurice fired his shotgun into the air, and the creature took off.

Terry pointed to the top of the ridge. "Lookee there," he said.

Something raced across the rocky crown on two legs, covered with brown, matted hair. Then it was gone.

Trouble Room

❖

Little Jim tossed the kitchen knife into the circle. Mumblety-peg was no fun by yourself. He flipped the knife up and over, wishing it wasn't his turn to keep watch for the Robisons. There was nothing to do by the cordwood pile except squish termites.

"Everyone else is probably havin' fun," he grumbled. Fun. It was something they did only when the Robisons weren't around. Otherwise, life was a prison.

He looked over at the girls playing jump rope with the clothesline. Three boys were playing cowboys, riding their broom horses. Those were things he longed to do but couldn't with his club foot.

Then he spied the wagon. "Here they come!" he called out.

The kids stopped their playing and ran back to their work stations. The girls raced down the clothesline hanging the shirts and pants. The boys got off their broom horses and began sweeping the walks.

Little Jim scurried over to the empty, rusting tub beside the barn, and beat out a message to the others who might be playing in the fields.

Tap, tap, tap.

"The meanies are comin'!"

Tap, tap, tap.

"Everyone get back to work!"

A chunky boy with badly chopped brown hair heard the sound and went running toward the orchard to warn the other boys who were eating apples instead of picking them.

"They comin'?" a mousy girl called out from the kitchen, her name painted on the back of her shirt to make washing and separating the orphans' clothes easier.

"On their way. Make sure that kitchen's clean," Little Jim said, knowing that Mrs. Robison would take the razor strap to anyone who wasn't doing chores.

The girl went into the kitchen and hid her paper dolls behind the ice chest. A little girl playing jacks scooped them up and stuck them under the bookcase in the front room.

Little Jim was frantic. *Where is she?* "Darleda, Darleda!" No answer. "Darleda, where are you?"

"Over here," she called back.

Little Jim limped over and found his best friend working on her poem. "They're almost here. Put that away."

She stuck the poem under her dress. "You better get back over to the barn. She warned you this mornin' not to shirk off."

"Hope she don't whip me again," said Little Jim. He was a lonely child who mothered up to Darleda, seeking protection. A mama's boy without a mama. Tension and fear of Mrs. Robison ate at his insides, giving him a constant stomachache that only an honest hug could cure.

"She won't," Darleda said, hugging him, trying to reassure the thin boy, but the truth was that there was no predicting what the woman would do.

The only thing for sure was that when Mrs. Robison was down on you, life was not good. Her eyes looked savage as a meat ax when she had your number. For a while her target was Stephen, one of the older boys. Then, for no reason, she began picking on Little Jim, making his bad-luck life even more miserable.

"Don't want to race no more," he said, taking Darleda's hand as they hurried back to their work stations.

Mrs. Robison's latest torture was making the crippled boy run out to the barn for a bucket of feed and giving him only one minute to do it. Timing him, she catcalled at him as the seconds ticked away. The moment he limped up the stairs, all tuckered out, she'd slap him for being seconds too slow.

Mealtime was the worst. Little Jim, who was small in size from the severe anemia and rickets he'd suffered when he was once placed in a bad foster home, had to sit on a thick dictionary to reach his food. The Robisons always gave him the smallest portions, saying that since he couldn't tote a full work load with his bad foot, they wouldn't waste good food on him.

"You better get over to the barn," Darleda said, releasing his hand. Jim lingered. "Darleda, you believe in angels?"

"Maybe." She watched the wagon come closer.

"Do you remember when we all used to be Mrs. Wilson's rainbow children?"

"I don't want to think about it. Things will never be that way again."

"I'm goin' to a better place," Jim said, smiling.

"You are?"

"Sure. God's gonna send an angel for me. Gonna come and take me to a better place."

"Take me with you."

"I will." He winked. "Wanna come with me later to feed the fawns?" Darleda was the only one he'd let in on his secret. He'd been feeding two motherless fawns in the old barn just off the orphanage property.

"If we don't get caught," she said conspiratorially.

Mrs. Robison looked around as they drove up, checking off a mental list of who had done what. Who needed punishing. The children moved forward to get in line, heads down, like zombies, not wanting to make eye contact. The Robisons always required that the orphans stand in line when they came back with supplies.

Darleda held back. Little Jim limped over and tugged at her blouse. "Darleda, come on, get in line."

"I hate them," she whispered.

"Don't let them hear you say that. They'll whip you good."

Little Jim got in line. "Did I get any mail?" he asked. It was his birthday, and Mrs. Wilson had promised before she left to send him a birthday card.

"No mail. Get in line and hold out your hands." Mrs. Robison's brutal gaze hid the churning in her stomach which seemed to stiffen her resolve.

Darleda was the last to get in line, which Mrs. Robison noted. She inspected her fingernails, whacking the back of the girl's hand.

"You've been biting your nails."

"No, I haven't."

"Yes, you have. Look at how ragged they are."

Darleda shook her head. "That's from weeding the rock garden."

"Don't contradict me," Mrs. Robison said harshly, raising her hand.

"I'll talk to her," John Robison said to his wife, saving Darleda from a stinging slap.

"You do that," Mrs. Robison snapped, moving down the line. Her husband watched, wondering what he should do. But he'd watched for so long that he felt paralyzed to do anything different.

"Each of you take a sack and march it back to the store room," commanded Mrs. Robison. As the children scurried to please her, she grabbed Darleda by the arm, her face turning as red as a barber's pole.

"And you, you've got to be locked up in the cold storage house."

"Why? What did I do?"

"You broke a dish. I found this piece under the ice box," the woman said, taking out a tiny sliver of china from her dress pocket.

"She didn't do it," Little Jim spoke up. "I . . ."

Darleda hushed the boy. She could take the punishment, but Little Jim couldn't. The cold storage room would make his club foot ache and swell up. "I did it. I'm sorry. I dropped it," she interrupted him.

"Sorry won't fix it. Ask Humpty Dumpty," Mrs. Robison answered.

Mr. Robison started to speak, then took a deep breath, turned around and walked away, avoiding the children's haunting eyes. Darleda was the only one with courage.

"Help us," Darleda whispered as he walked by.

They locked eyes for a brief moment. It was unsettling, forcing him to close the distance he'd put between himself and his wife's actions.

Mrs. Robison stepped forward and pinched Darleda's arm. "Don't be askin' for help."

Darleda didn't cry out even though the nails broke through her skin. The few seconds seemed to stop in time as the electricity of hatred built between them. The air was charged like a static-filled room.

"Why can't you be nice to us?" Darleda asked.

"Nice, huh?" She looked at Darleda's long, golden hair bouncing sunbeams across her shoulders. "Nice hair, but a bit too long."

"No, my father likes it this way."

Mrs. Robison flicked the shoulder-length hair around. "Your father's abandoned you. He's never coming back, Darley."

"My name's Darleda."

Mrs. Robison froze. "I said Darleda. And your father's not coming back."

"He is."

"No. He isn't. And soon you'll be ready for adoption so it's time you had a haircut." She smiled. "Something fashionable."

"No, please," Darleda whimpered.

The other children moved into the shadows, not wanting to be noticed next.

"John, bring me the kerosene," Mrs. Robison demanded.

Darleda shivered. They used the kerosene once a month—they poured it on the children's heads to kill lice. Darleda watched as one child after the other bent over and had the stinging chemical scrubbed into their scalps.

"Now, John, go get me the scissors." Mrs. Robison looked at the girl. "Sit on the stump. Right there."

Snip, snip.

The children watched in silence as she brutally cut the girl's beautiful hair.

Snip, snip.

The golden locks fell in uneven clumps. Darleda didn't move, didn't cry out, just sat simmering with hatred for the woman who was doing this. The air was hot in her lungs. She wanted to grab the woman's face and squeeze until it shattered. *You can't keep me here. You can't,* Darleda thought, over and over.

She swallowed the seeds of bitterness. In her mind they were already bearing fruit of sweet revenge. For the first time in her life she knew what hate was. *Your time will come. It will come,* she told herself.

"Well, young lady, now you look perfect, ready for Adoption Day," Mrs. Robison smirked, admiring her handiwork.

It looked awful.

Little Jim ached for his friend. "You look . . . look good," he said to Darleda. But she knew he was lying.

"And now, it's time for your punishment," Mrs. Robison sneered, pulling Darleda along by the ear. Suddenly she stopped, gulping for air.

Boom, boom, boom.

Sarah Robison counted off the seconds between the pounding in her brain, reaching for another packet of aspirin powder. She had thought that by cutting off her hair Darleda wouldn't look so much like the daughter she'd lost. It didn't work.

Boom, boom, boom.

The pounding was so loud that she thought the world could hear it. Reaching frantically for her purse, she took out a white packet. Choking down the aspirin powder, she looked at the children and saw the fear in their eyes. Like they had just uncovered a rattlesnake's nest.

Little Jim snuck up and whispered, "The angel's are comin' soon, Darleda."

"I don't know if angels even know we exist," Darleda whispered back.

"They do. Don't lose hope. My angel's gonna come."

"Get away from her!" Mrs. Robison screamed.

The other children watched the strong-willed girl being pushed toward the feared punishment room where the cured hams were hung. Darleda took a breath and looked at Mrs. Robison before the door was slammed shut. "What you're doin' isn't right. When my father comes back, he'll bring trouble down on your head."

The woman laughed without smiling. "Your father's either dead or long gone. When will you accept the fact that he's abandoned you?"

"He hasn't."

"He has. A year's gone by so I'm gonna put you up for adoption—if anyone wants you," she sneered, slamming the door. The pain between her eyes was blinding.

Darleda pounded against the rough-planked door. "My father's coming back to take me to Denver! I know he is!"

"Your father went back to find himself a wife. Paint a pretty picture of Denver to some other girl."

Darleda was silent. She couldn't help questioning her faith that her father was coming back.

"That's right," Mrs. Robison continued. "I bet your father's wedded some young thing and is already in Denver, workin' on another family. He's forgotten about you. That's the way men are." The sound of Darleda's crying pleased her. "Think about that."

"We used to all be rainbow children," Little Jim whispered to himself.

Mrs. Robison quick-stepped back to him and pinched his arm. "There's no pot of gold at the end of a rainbow. Only work. Hard work. Go clean out the barn!"

Her husband walked over to her. "Come lie down, Sarah. Take another powder. You'll feel better."

"The children need discipline. Discipline!" she shouted.

26

Trespasser

❖

The dime novel held fast in Larry's pocket, rubbing against the saddle. Lightnin' tugged at the tall grass, trying to munch it, but there wasn't time to stop. Larry was on an across-lots course, determined to cut straight to his destination no matter what the obstacles.

He looked around, thinking through the story in his book. The Ozarks dissolved. In his mind he was back to long ago, when shiny, armored knights journeyed across the countryside on prancing steeds, shields raised, on their way to rescue damsels. Larry saw himself saluting King Arthur, riding off to do battle. Who he was going to fight, was unknown. He was ready, that's all that counted.

His father had warned him to keep off the orphanage property when Mrs. Robison had complained about his trespassing. Larry had given his word, he understood that, but it was something he had to do. Felt driven to do. It was what a good knight would do. It wasn't anything he could explain to his father, to his brother, or to anyone else. Maybe not even to himself. It was just a feeling that something wasn't right and that a girl who was prettier than a hill full of spring flowers was up there and needed his help.

He saw himself charging across their property, lance pointed, valiantly challenging the Dark Hats on their devil-black horses. In his mind he saw the fury of the clash as he knocked the dark knight off his horse, then turned to face the mean woman. He hesitated, wondering if he should charge forward. The dream dissolved without Larry's being forced to confront his father's teachings about not hitting girls.

At the edge of the orphanage property, Larry ignored the "Keep Out—No Trespassing" sign and rode along the path that he and Terry had followed to spy on the orphans on their earlier trips. Honeysuckle mingled in the wild grapevines, but Larry didn't stop to suck out the sweet juice. His pulse was racing. Darleda was somewhere up ahead. He picketed his horse in a natural brush pen, then crept quietly until he was close to the buildings. He watched the dark-hatted woman yell at the children, calling them terrible names. He waited until the Robisons had gone into their sleeping quarters, then moved forword. Keeping close to the trees, he made his way slowly forward.

When he got to the edge of the barn, Larry jumped with fright when a voice behind him asked, "What's that in your pocket?"

"What?" He turned and saw Little Jim. The boy looked very frail, like he'd been surviving on just bread and milk.

"Thought you were my angel, but I 'member you now. You're one of the town boys. Preacher's kid, ain't ya?"

Larry nodded.

"What's that in your pocket?" Little Jim repeated.

"I'm Larry. It's a dime novel." Larry took it out and unrolled it as if to prove the truth of what he said.

Little Jim flipped through the pages. "You read this stuff?"

"Yeah. I like to read."

"What you doin' here?"

"Just lookin' 'round, that's all," Larry shrugged, sticking the knight's story back into his trousers.

"Me, why I'd have no reason to look 'round here if I didn't live here. You'd be better off tap-dancin' for the devil than gettin' caught by ol' Mrs. Robison."

"Why do *you* stay?" Larry asked.

Little Jim shrugged. "Ain't easy to go when you don't know where you are. But if I did get away, I'd never look back. Just ride west till my pony got hisself wet in the Pa-si-fick Ocean."

Larry grinned. "What's your name? I don't remember seeing you before."

"Jim. Jim Duncan. But everyone here calls me Little Jim seein's how small I am and all." Then he shrugged. "But it's better than bein' called Crip or Clubfoot like I was in St. Louis."

"How'd you end up here?"

"Not sure, really. All I knows is that I don't remember ever havin' folks, no ma or pa or anything. Just orphan home folks. Think I was left on the church steps."

"How'd you get here?"

"Man and woman who took me from St. Louis said I couldn't work my load. Couldn't pull my weight on their farm." Little Jim looked off, remembering. "They thought I was a slave or somethin'. Like I was lookin' to be worked to death."

Larry looked down, embarrassed that he was part of a good family. "Someone will want you on Adoption Day."

"No one wants a crippled boy."

"What's wrong with your foot? You got the old disease or somethin'?" Larry asked, remembering the old man in town with the arthritic leg.

"Don't think they call it that. My leg's not the same length as the other, and my foot kinda turns out crooked like."

"That's too bad." Those weren't the best words to say, but it was all Larry could think of.

"Say, have you ever seen a monster?"

"A what?" Larry asked.

"A monster. The Missouri Mud Monster we heard Mr. Mead, the carpenter man, speakin' about. Said it's been comin' 'round his place, rootin' through the garbage."

"Just a story. That's all I think it is."

"But I seen tracks."

"Where?"

"Up near our garbage pit. And I smelled a stink so bad that I thought the devil hisself had poked out of the ground to air hisself out."

Larry chuckled. "You musta had beans for supper." He looked around for Darleda.

"You lookin' for someone?"

"Maybe."

"Maybe who?"

"A girl with golden hair," Larry said softly.

Jim pointed to the cold storage shed.

"What's she doin' in there?" Larry asked.

"'Cause she wouldn't rat." Little Jim explained about the broken plate and how Mrs. Robison had it in for Darleda.

"If she sits in that cold room all night, she'll freeze to death," Larry protested.

"There's empty sacks and such in there. She may be cold, but Darleda won't die. She's gonna live until her daddy comes back for her."

"Where's her daddy?"

"In New York."

"Why won't he come get her?"

"Mrs. Robison says he abandoned Darleda."

Larry looked at the cold storage room, wishing he could talk to the pretty girl. "What's she like?"

"She's mean as a snake, cold as Mr. Winter's frosty bite, and sour as a two-day early green apple."

"Do tell! She is?" Larry gasped.

"That's right." Little Jim went on describing Mrs. Robison. "Why, if'n you were to go hold her hand, she'd pinch it off. And if you was to smile, she'd slap your face. And if you were to get sick and wish someone would just sit by your side and be nice to you, well, let me tell you, that ol' girl would sit down, sure 'nough, but she'd sit down to torment you to no end."

"Darleda's like that?"

Little Jim laughed. "No, I'm talkin' 'bout mean ol' Mrs. Robison. The only witch I know who don't ride a broom." Then he squinted up his face, trying to suppress a nervous grin. "Do you like Darleda?"

"I ain't never even talked to her."

"I seen the way you're lookin' over, wonderin' if she's all right. You're gee-gaw over her, ain't you?"

"I ain't gee-gaw over *no* girl."

"You cotton to her, don'tcha?" Little Jim winked.

Larry blushed like a plum. "Just worried 'bout her bein' locked up there, that's all."

Little Jim fluttered his lips. "And I got two good feet. That's okay. You don't got to say so. It's written on your face. *All* over your face."

Larry blushed, not wanting to hear any more. "I'm gonna go over and see how she's doin'. Cover for me, okay?"

Pointing to the back corner, Little Jim whispered, "Just move that block of wood with the knothole on the end. You can talk to her there. That's how we slip each other food when we're in the trouble house."

Larry moved away. Little Jim wanted to ask more questions about the Mud Monster. He didn't get many chances to talk to other children besides the orphans. "Hope that kid comes back again." Then he remembered that he'd forgotten to tell Larry about Darleda's haircut.

Larry crept over to the back wall of the cold storage room and moved the block with the knothole. It was wedged in tight so he had to wiggle it with both hands. When he finally slipped it out, he took a breath, wondering what to say or what to do. With his mama dead, he didn't know much about women and less about girls. He looked into the room and saw Darleda staring back at him. He wanted to speak, wanted to say something, but his heart was beating so fast, so darn fast, that his words were lost. He could hardly breathe let alone speak, relying on stirred up boy-things inside him that came out of the blue. Moving him along heartbeat by heartbeat.

"Hi," she said, embarrassed fingers fretting about her rough-chopped hair.

Even though her hair was a mess, Larry didn't notice. Her smile warmed his face. Made him blush. Her voice was like angel's breath to his ears. His throat was dry. He struggled to speak.

"Hi," he croaked, his voice breaking. Just seeing her face made him dizzy.

"She did this to me."

"What?"

"Cut my hair."

"Oh gosh," he whispered, his voice pained, suddenly noticing her hair and how it bothered her. "You had such pretty hair."

"She hated it. Hates me."

"But your hair. Why?"

Darleda shrugged. "It'll grow back."

He remembered Sherry's first candy bag and dug into his pocket to retrieve it. He handed it to Darleda shyly. "Want some candy?"

"Thanks," she said, reaching for the crumpled bag in his hand.

When their fingers touched, Larry held on to the bag, wondering what the tingle was that was racing up his spine, shooting through his soul. Why did he feel this way? It was all a wonderful mystery that made him feel dizzy. He could have cared less if she were bald. All he knew was that she was the prettiest girl he'd ever set eyes on.

"What's your name?" she asked.

He swallowed hard, trying to find his voice. "Larry. Larry Youngun."

"My name's Darleda Jackson. I'm not an orphan. My father's coming back to get me. I know he is."

"Where is he?"

"He went back to New York to get his mother."

"Why did he leave you here?"

"My mother died on the way to Denver."

Larry nodded. "My ma's dead too."

"You ever been to Denver?"

"Nope. Been to St. Louis and traveled once to Florida, but never much west."

"I'm gonna live in Denver. See the snowcapped mountains every morning. My dad says the air is so crispy fresh that you can feel God's breath blowin' over ice blocks."

Larry hesitated then asked, "You sure your pa's comin' back?"

"I know it in my heart."

Larry didn't know what to say, so he just sat there looking at the most beautiful face in the world. He wasn't sure why he wanted to protect her, why he wanted to do battle for her like the good knights he'd read about, but he did. *I'd slay dragons for her. I'd fight an army to protect her.*

Darleda ate another piece of candy. "I used to sit where you are, reading by the last light of day."

"What'd you read?"

"Anything. Magazines usually. But she found where I had them under my bed and threw them away. I hid a few, though."

"Read this," he said, handing her his dime novel.

"What's it about?"

"Knights and stuff like that."

"Thanks." She smiled, looking at the colorful fighting scene on the cover.

Larry was lost in her smile. Her damsel smile. There was nothing he wouldn't have done for her. No battles he wouldn't fight.

"You should keep an eye out for the ogre," she said cautiously.

"Who?"

"Mrs. Robison."

"I'll be okay. A kid with a bad foot's watchin' for her."

"Little Jim. He's my friend."

Larry watched her turn the pages. Nothing about her was too perfect. He'd never felt this way about a girl before in his whole life.

27

Caught

❖

Inside the main orphanage building, a call came in from Mrs. Wilson. It was a terse, short conversation. Mrs. Robison didn't feel well, didn't want to talk about Adoption Day or the upcoming Board meeting. She wanted to be left alone.

"No, you can't speak to the children," she said abruptly.

"But why? I just wanted to wish Little Jim happy birthday."

"I run this place. Outside thoughts only hurt them worse."

"You can't be serious," Mrs. Wilson exclaimed.

"I am!"

"Why didn't you write me that Darleda had died? As a member of the Board I should have been informed."

"I was too busy taking care of the children."

Boom, boom, boom. A spell was coming on.

"Too busy? To tell me that one of my girls died? Her father needs a final photograph. Did you send him one?" Mrs. Wilson was worried. Something didn't seem right.

It was common practice at the turn of the century, when fewer than half the children survived beyond the age of ten, for a photographer to take a final deathbed picture of a child.

"We didn't take one."

"I'm afraid I'll have to bring this up at the Board meeting."

Boom, boom, boom. Sarah's head felt like it was splitting open. She was silent.

"A death portrait would have been the decent thing to do," Mrs. Wilson said over the crackling line.

Boom, boom, boom. All Sarah wanted to do was get off the phone. "Answer me, Mrs. Robison. Are you there?"

Silence.

"Are you there?"

Gripping the phone, wishing she could smash the receiver against the wall, Mrs. Robison spoke slowly. "I'm sorry that the girl died and that we didn't have the money for a death portrait. But she's dead and buried so there's nothing we can do about it now. It's upset us all. Can't you understand that?"

That caught Mrs. Wilson off guard. "Yes . . . yes I can." Then she remembered why she'd called. "Have you told the other Board members about your financial problems? Would you like me to mention it at the meeting?"

Mrs. Robison gritted her teeth. "No. And I don't think you should come to the meeting. You come back, and you'll just upset the kids."

"But . . ."

"I really think we should call off the Adoption Day and wait another year until the children are ready."

"Ready? Orphans are always ready to be adopted." Mrs. Wilson was incredulous.

"Their manners need improving."

"Aren't you being too harsh? Maybe I can talk with them, calm them down if you're having trouble."

"You're not welcome here anymore," Mrs. Robison said, hanging up the phone. *If she comes back, she'll ruin everything. What should I do?*

In Springfield, Mrs. Wilson knew what she had to do. She had to get to her children. "There's something very wrong with that woman," she told her sister.

John Robison looked out and saw the Youngun boy crouched by the storage house. "We got a boy trespassin'. That Youngun boy," he said to his wife.

Sarah went to the window. "What's he doin' here?" she hissed sharply. The pain was contorting her face. The inner rage was ready to explode.

"I'll tell him to leave."

"No!" she snapped, grabbing his arm. "You get him. Hold him for me."

John started to speak, then thought again. His wife was on the edge, teetering. She could go either way. "Calm down a bit," he said gently. "I'll handle this."

"Just get that boy," she gasped, pushing against her temples. The pain was intense. All she could hear was the pounding in her head as she staggered from the room.

Larry's fingers crept toward Darleda's hand that was playing in the sunlight that danced on the edge where the block of wood had been removed. *Just a touch. Just hold her hand for a minute.* He worried that she'd hear his beating heart through his shirt.

Darleda heard the drain pipe tapping and put down the dime novel. "You better leave," she warned.

"Why?"

"The witch is comin'! Run before she grabs you!"

Before he could turn around, he felt the firm grip on his arm. "Trespassin's against the law," Mrs. Robison hissed, pinching his arm as she dragged him back to her husband who stood waiting like a school-yard bully. She was taking her frustrations over the call from Mrs. Wilson out on the boy.

"Let him go," Darleda shouted through the hole.

"Get off me!" Larry said, but the dark-hatted woman's nails dug deeper into his arm. "You're hurtin' me."

"Too bad," she grunted, pulling him.

Little Jim limped along, talking fast, trying to help Larry out. "He got lost. Was askin' how to get back to town. I told him Darleda was the only one who knew the way back."

Mrs. Robison snickered. "Little club foot, I think you're a liar."

Little Jim stopped. "Honest, that's the truth."

"No it's not. Go scrub down the barn."

"What are you really doin' out here?" Mr. Robison asked Larry.

Larry struggled until he'd pushed Mrs. Robison's pinching, sharp finger nails off his arm. "I just came visitin', that's all." A clump of golden hair near a stump caught his eye.

"Visitors don't sneak. They ride straight up. Is that what you're sayin' you done, boy?" Mr. Robison asked.

"No sir. I just rode around, wonderin' what the kids here were doin'. Wonderin' if they wanted to come play ball or somethin'," he said, pretending to adjust his boot while he palmed the curl of golden hair.

Mrs. Robison moved quickly, anger flickering behind her eyes like lightning. "And that's why you were peekin' and sneakin', talkin' to that girl in the trouble house?" she hissed, pinching his arm again.

"I wasn't meanin' no harm." Larry winced, not wanting to cry out in pain, knowing that Darleda would hear him. The woman's nails cut deeper into his skin.

"You're a lyin' boy who's been sniffin' 'round like some moon-struck dog," Mrs. Robison began.

Larry watched her eyes glaze over, but he didn't cry because knights didn't cry. No matter what they accused him of, no matter how disappointed his father would be when they marched him up to his front door, Larry didn't care. He'd touched an angel. An earth angel who needed his help. And that was all he could think about.

"Take this boy to his father. Demand that he whip him for trespassing on our property," Mrs. Robison said to her husband.

Larry suddenly saw the consequences of trespassing. Of breaking his word to his father. *Pa's sick. He don't need trouble like this.*

"I'm sorry. I won't come back," he said quickly.

"You said that the last time."

"Honest. No need to go gettin' my pa all upset. He's been sick."

"Too bad. You should have thought about that before you came back around here," she sneered.

"I won't come back."

Mrs. Robison squeezed Larry's arm. "Get in the wagon."

"What about my horse?"

"Tie it up on the back."

Larry walked slowly to get Lightnin', wondering if he should just take off. But it would do no good. They were adults and would confront his father sometime. It was better to get it over with.

Mrs. Robison's head ached, her deeply lined forehead barely able to hold back the thunder trapped between her ears. She took her husband aside and said, "Mrs. Wilson's coming to visit."

"So?"

She spat her words with an acid tone. "So, she'll go talking around to the kids and town folks, the Board members too, and things will look bad."

"What do you think we should do?" John Robison asked, looking around at the kids, suddenly seeing each one as a danger to them. "Why don't we go to a big city, find you a doctor, and . . ."

Mrs. Robison shook her head. "No. I'm gonna get better if I stay right here."

"But the Board meeting's comin' up."

"You handle it. Make up something. Tell them I'm sick."

John ignored her slip of the tongue. "No."

"Tell them I've got the flu."

"What about Adoption Day? We gotta do something. These kids need a chance," John Robison argued.

With a cutting glance, Sarah chopped the air with her hand. "Once they're disciplined they'll have their chance."

John shook his head, the saliva drying in his mouth. "It's time to go. Move on. I can feel it in my soul."

Sarah dropped her head, knowing it was true. "If we go we'll take Darleda with us."

He looked toward the trouble house. "You'd have to tie her to the back of a wagon. She'll never go with you. She's not Darley. Darley's dead and gone."

"I know she's not Darley. But I have a right to a daughter."

John frowned. "That girl doesn't like you. You can see it in her eyes. It's because of the way you treat her."

"I tried to love her. Tried to replace her father," Sarah whined.

"But that wasn't right. She has a father."

"No she doesn't. He's never coming back. After a year Darleda can be put up for adoption. It's the law. And I want to adopt her."

"Sarah, I don't think we should."

"I've made up my mind."

Sarah went into her sewing room and took out the dolly that had belonged to her daughter. She held it up by the foot, swinging it back and forth. Then she slammed it against the table and went to her sewing kit and took out a pair of scissors. First the dress. Then the yarn hair. Sarah clipped off the feet and arms of the doll until there was nothing left.

"No one can help me. No one," she moaned.

"What you doin' in there, Sarah?" her husband called out.

"Just thinking about the children," she whispered, clutching the scissors.

Passing Through

❖

Darleda huddled in the cold room, covered with burlap sacks for warmth, wondering what she'd done to deserve all this punishment. Fresh sweat formed on her lip, on her forehead. Even though the temperature was cold, she felt feverish. She prayed that if Little Jim's angel came, that it would take her away too. A flash of understanding about how bad things really were came over her.

On the other side of Missouri, near the Illinois line, Robert Jackson was having second thoughts. He didn't have enough money to buy another ticket if he missed the train. He'd budgeted to the penny to get to Denver. Renting a horse to ride to Mansfield would stretch him thin. There'd be meals to give up. *Wouldn't have much time to ride from the depot at the Arkansas fork to Mansfield and back. Hardly enough time to pay my respects to Darleda's grave.*

He had a day to make his mind up, but it seemed better to just pass Mansfield by and head toward Denver. To begin life over in the Rockies. He didn't need any more pain piled on agony.

Unfolding the death notice, he read it again.

Darleda Jackson died July 17, 1908, of diphtheria and is buried in the Mansfield cemetery.

It was stark, cold. He couldn't imagine Darleda, who had so much life to give, lying in the ground. *Got to say my last good-byes. Tell her how sorry I am for not takin' her with me.*

The conductor walked by, telling everyone that the train was running late.

Maybe I can come back out here one day. See her grave. And Caroline and the baby's too. Can't miss this train. Got to think about the future, not the past.

It made all the sense in the world to by pass Darleda's grave and go begin his future in Denver. *There's mountains up there where a man can get lost. Lose his past. Begin fresh. That's what I need. That's what I'm gonna do. Darleda would understand if she were still alive.*

29

Wild Tale

❖

Dr. George told the sheriff a second time what he'd seen, omitting the part about the chicken grease smudged on his glasses. "I tell you what, that was a monster sure as I'm sitting here."

"You saw it clear as day?"

"As I'm seeing you."

Sheriff Peterson stood in the middle of a path worn through the varnish which led from the front door to his desk. He looked skeptical but knew that word would spread like wildfire from the saloon to the back road farms, then every drinker and superstitious person around would be seeing things. He could hear the phone lines crackling, old ladies thinking dogs were monsters and the neighbor kids were vampires come to kill them. Still, he knew that Dr. George was a teetotaler and a truth-telling man.

"Describe this thing again," the sheriff said. He listened as Dr. George's tale grew taller with each retelling. "What do you think it was?" he asked, stroking his long-jawed chin.

Dr. George hesitated. He didn't want to say it was the boogeyman. Folks would have a laugh for weeks if word got around about that. "Some kind of woods monster. That's all I can call it."

"Was he eight foot or ten?"

"Somewhere around there. He was big, I know that for sure. I think you ought to go get a posse up."

"Uh-huh. And you say he looked like a sheepdog with matted hair?"

Dr. George nodded.

"And he stank to high heaven?"

"I told you, it was like a big stink bug covered with hair that came running after me, trying to kill me. I was so close I could touch it." Dr. George left out the part about not having his glasses on when the creature climbed up and covered his eyes.

"Dr. George, I've been hearin' stories 'bout ghosts and demons comin' out of the woods for years. I just don't have time to believe in such things."

"I didn't say it was a ghost. I am not a country bumpkin. I know what I saw."

"How 'bout you writin' down everythin' you saw. I'll be outside. I need some air to think 'bout this."

Dr. George held the piece of paper in his hand. He started to write, then scratched it out. *Can't say that I really didn't see it clearly. That I'd chicken-greased up my glasses. Sheriff would make me out to be some kind of fool. No one would want me operating on them.*

But he had to write something, so he began an account of a ten-foot monster that attacked him:

A True Statement of What I Saw

On the north road, at the bend in the woods near the swamp, I had a flat tire. When I finished changing it, I saw a ten-foot-tall creature. I stood my ground and scared the creature away, but as I drove away, it charged my automobile and tried to climb onto the back, to kill me, but I swatted it until it fell off and ran howling away.

Dr. George nodded, reading it over. Then he signed it.

Peterson stood on the sidewalk outside, knowing the panic this would set off after the newspaper got its hands on the story. He had heard the tales over the years about creatures of all sizes and descriptions who supposedly roamed throughout Missouri. *Story's been 'round since Indian days 'bout them things. Sounds like some big drunk logger that fell in a privy and now is tryin' to find a bath.*

He remembered back some ten years before when there'd been talk of a Lizard Man, a half lizard, half human thing that was supposedly running wild along the Mississippi. Some of the local boys had taken to hunting it and managed to shoot a couple of cows and dogs in the process.

Peterson was a reasonable man with feet-on-the-ground common sense. "Everything has an explanation. There's no mysteries left. The experts have an answer for everything," he mused.

He walked over to the doctor's automobile and saw the scratches along the back. He sniffed at the seat and scrunched his nose at the awful smell. Caught on the back light was a tuft of thick, matted animal hair.

"Sheriff, got somethin' to tell you."

Peterson turned and saw Henry Mead holding a dog collar, rubbing his forehead. Mead's brain still ached from the mine fire. He told the sheriff about Rufus, about the attack at the mine, and what the fishermen had seen. "You gotta call up some boys," Mead said. "We gotta kill this creature before it attacks someone again. It's the Mud Monster. I'll swear to that."

"Henry, now don't go startin' rumors. Mud Monster's nothin' but an old Indian tale."

"What I saw was alive as day."

"You probably saw a bear."

"Sheriff, I've been huntin' these woods for sixty years. I know a bear when I see one, and that weren't no bear. It weren't like anythin' I've ever seen. Part cat, part man . . . if you can call anythin' that looks like that a man."

"You'll get the boys 'round here all worked up, grabbin' at their hog legs and rifles, shootin' everythin' in sight."

Mead went face-to-face. "Sheriff, someone's gonna get killed 'fore they get a chance to be worked up."

"Just think 'bout what I'm tellin' you."

"Your thinkin's gettin' in the way of our doin' somethin' about this thing. It's got to be killed."

30

Reward

❖

By the time Henry Mead had finished telling his tales around town, the Mud Monster had eaten not only his dog Rufus, but half the cows in his barn. He had fought it bare-handed as the creature tried to bite his throat. After two drinks, his exaggerations grew until the night he'd spent behind the rocks had turned into the Alamo with Mead barely surviving the hours of attacks.

Tippy's Saloon was a blue-smoke-filled sauna of sweating, poker-playing men sipping cheap whiskey and stale beer. Cooped-up smells of farmyards, animals, and dung-clotted boots hung in the room, unmoved by the clickety-clack fan struggling on the ceiling. A wall of bottle spirits for the men to abuse themselves with twinkled from the wall sconce lights. Word had spread about what happened to Mead, and men had been pushing steadily through the bat wing doors for the past hour.

"You boys best gather 'round if you want to hear me out," Mead said. The sullen, florid-faced men moved toward him.

"Better not be a bunch of bunkum and claptrap," said a jumpy-eyed one, dressed sharp like a dandy with thick lips and skin so dry that he looked like he was about to shed. He pushed back the turkey flap of a neck that covered the knot of his tie, grumbling that he was wasting his time in the jerkwater town.

"Come over and listen," wheezed out a retired logger.

"Better be good," the dandy said, scratching at the skin flakes on his arm. He knocked back his drink, adjusted his string tie and sauntered over.

The barkeep made a face. "Someone's been eatin' too many pickles. Go outside next time and belch your brains out."

When things had quieted down and the clatter of poker chips and empty glasses being racked had ended, Mead sat in a corner, telling how he'd fought the monster bare-handed, going face-to-face with a demon. His voice was low, quiet and deep, forcing the men to lean forward to heard his words. His eyes told the story with ice pick glances. His emotion was bow-string taut, pulling back farther and farther until he let loose with the fight in the dark.

The dog collar in his hand fueled his anger. "I tell you, boys," he said, nodding for another drink, "it looked like a human skeleton with red eyes and teeth as sharp as a bobcat."

"How many arms it have?" asked the bent-over barfly with a rat-squeak voice.

"Least six. Maybe more."

A fat-jowled, weather-burned man with a three-day beard pounded the bar. "Gimme another. This boy's story is slicker'n you know what." He belched, clearing his throat. "You're lucky to be alive."

"You sure you ain't sellin' us wolf tickets?" another called out.

Mead shook his head; then grinned, adding to the deep lines around his eyes. "I'd dance on the devil's coffin. It's all true." The ruddy faces in the room were frightened and angered by the cheap alcohol.

"I don't know if I should be sayin' this, but in that cave, wrapped in finger-thick vines that came up from the bowels of the earth, were bones," Mead said.

"What kind of bones?" asked a farmer in greasy overalls with an Ozark twang in his voice. The clock chimed on the wall, but no one looked or noticed that the farmer poured salt on the bar and threw some over his shoulder for good luck.

"People bones. Human bones. Arms, legs, ribs. It was a terrible sight. And there were snakes, Lord, you shoulda seen the snakes crawlin' through the skulls, hissin' their tongues out."

Mead looked around conspiratorially. He was working himself up into such a frenzy that breathing was hard. The men around him could all make a wooden Indian blush with their cussing, but they were sitting on the edge of their stools, listening like kids at a campfire, enjoying the tingle under their skin. Even the cook came out from the kitchen, quietly shelling peas, hanging on every word.

Gesturing with his hands to draw them closer, Mead whispered, "I don't know if I should be tellin' you 'bout this, but the creature changed shapes. One minute it was a hairy devil, runnin' on humanlike legs, and the next minute it was like a dragon-lion. Just thinkin' 'bout it makes my bones chilled." He looked each of the men in the face. "Don't think any of you should go huntin' this thing without makin' your peace with your Maker. Whatever's up in those hills ain't human." The cook spilled the shelled peas all over the floor.

"You sure you ain't just passin' air on us, old timer?" a young buck called out.

"Swear on my mother's grave and all the apple jack you can drink." Mead scratched his chin. "And remember, boys, this thing's over ten feet tall and eats dogs and cows. So it'll probably eat one of you if you ain't careful."

"I hear it's got fire-red eyes and breathes smoke," shouted one of the loggers, who was missing his front teeth from an accident at the mill.

Mead had drunk too much and agreed. "And sometimes it has four arms that move like a dragon."

"Nothin' that a bullet won't stop," Tippy said. The crowd turned. Tippy, the owner of the saloon, offered five hundred dollars to the man who shot the creature if he could have it mounted in the saloon. Tapping his cigar ash onto the floor, he motioned to everyone to crowd around.

"Here's the money, boys," Tippy said, holding up five one-hundred-dollar bills. "This ain't confederate money. It's good as gold for the man who brings me the monster's head." The roomful of red-eyed drunks pressed forward, ogle eycing the crisp bills.

It wouldn't be a night to let your dog run loose.

31

Second Chance

❖

Rev. Youngun heard the wagon approach. It was far enough away to give him time to get his strength up to make it to the porch. The fresh air felt good. He shook his head, thinking about how the hoot owl had scared him. His grin faded when he saw Larry sitting beside Mr. Robison on the wagon, neither one talking. He knew Larry had gotten himself into something over at the orphanage. Bad news was coming.

The dark-hatted man pulled the wagon to a halt in front of the porch. He got down and shook hands with Rev. Youngun. "Sorry to be comin' over without callin' when you're sick, Rev. Youngun."

"Hi, Pa," Larry said weakly, already sorry that he brought more troubles on his sickly pa's shoulders.

"Mr. Robison. Is there something wrong?" Rev. Youngun asked, holding back a cough.

Mr. Robison hesitated. "We caught your son trespassin' on our property, and I wanted to come talk face-to-face."

Larry sat silently, listening to Mr. Robison put a bad spin on what he'd done. Larry kept his anger lodged in his throat. The events grew by leaps and bounds until what he was hearing sounded like a story from the *Police Gazette*. He kept the lock of hair clenched in his fist like it was the most valuable thing in the world. When his father finally asked him to speak, all Larry could say was, "That ain't what happened."

"Are you calling me a liar, boy?" Mr. Robison said, gritting his teeth.

Larry looked at the older man. "I'm just sayin' that you're not describin' what happened the way it happened. Take that as you want to, but I won't be admittin' to somethin' I didn't do."

"Did you come on our property?"

Larry nodded.

"Did you sneak around among our buildings?"

Larry again nodded.

"And did you try to talk to that girl in the trouble house?"

"Did you, son?" his father asked. He reached for the porch rail to steady himself. He felt weak, like he needed to lie down.

"You all right, Rev. Youngun?" Mr. Robison asked.

"Just a touch of flu," he whispered. "Larry, did you break your promise?"

"Pa, I went on their property. I was just curious. I meant no one no harm."

"Maybe I should come back another time," Robison said.

"No, it's all right."

"My wife said you were going to tell the children to keep away from the orphanage."

"I did."

"Rev. Youngun, I think your son needs to get well-acquainted with the end of a belt."

"If he needs discipline, I'll handle it my way."

"Discipline, that's what keeps a boy from goin' bad, Rev. Youngun."

"Why'd you go back?" Rev. Youngun asked Larry.

"Just wanted to see if the kids wanted to play." It was a white lie and Larry immediately felt bad.

"Our children don't need to play with other kids," Mr. Robison said bluntly.

"But they used to come to town, and we'd all play ball," Larry said, wishing he could tell his dad about the girl. "But now they've got 'em locked up like jailbirds, cleanin', washin', beatin' 'em and treatin' 'em like they was convicts, not little kids."

"Rev. Youngun, I can assure you that our children are being reared in the way of the Lord as we understand it."

"Lord doesn't say to beat 'em. No, Pa."

Mr. Robison sighed. "The boy exaggerates. All children need discipline. You know that, Reverend. We just can't have kids and whatnots peekin' into our windows, scaring the girls and . . ."

"I didn't, Pa, I swear. That place is like a prison."

Mr. Robison laughed. "Not hardly. Prisons have walls of stone."

"Not all of them, believe me, Pa." Larry couldn't understand why his father didn't stand up for him, right there on the spot. Put this mean man in his place and ride over with him to the orphanage and save them all. Then his father broke down coughing.

Mr. Robison nudged Larry to get down off the wagon. "Son, you were on our property. All I'm askin' is that you leave us alone. Is that too much to ask, Rev. Youngun?"

"No," he said hoarsely, clearing his throat. "You're being very decent about this. I'll make sure that my boy doesn't come on your property again. Larry, apologize to Mr. Robison."

Larry hesitated. *Pa's listenin' with old ears. He's believin' that man over me.*

"Larry, I said to apologize to Mr. Robison."

"Sorry," he said quickly, though in his heart he wasn't sorry. He was mad at the false coloring of his actions and more determined than ever to go back and talk to Darleda. He was also miffed by his father's lack of action on his behalf.

"Tell Mrs. Robison that it won't happen again," Rev. Youngun said.

Robison started to speak, wanting to take this man of the cloth aside to talk about his wife. He'd never opened up to anyone before. Now, knowing that his wife's spells were getting worse and worse, he couldn't drink himself away this time. Couldn't distance himself any longer from the sins he knew were being committed. Sins of child abuse, which he knew were in his power to prevent. *I've got to do something, but what? They'll send her to an institution if I tell her secret.*

Rev. Youngun had seen the look before. The man was burdened with troubles. "Is there something you want to say?"

"She'll appreciate hearin' that. That's all," Mr. Robison said quietly, unable to look directly at the minister.

"Larry, why don't you wait inside." Rev. Youngun waited until Larry had closed the door, then took a tentative step down the stairs. "Mr. Robison, is there something you want to talk about? To unburden yourself of?"

Fluttering his lips, John Robison shrugged. "I'm not much of a Bible man if that's what you're wondering."

"I'm not going to preach you a sermon. I just thought maybe there was something bothering you."

John Robison looked out toward the fields, took a long breath, and held it. Exhaling, he shook his head. "No, there's nothing I need to speak about. You better get yourself some rest. You look weak as a kitten."

"If you need to talk, call me. I've got a good ear."

"I appreciate that offer." Without another word, John Robison walked back to his wagon, climbed up, and rode off.

When Mr. Robison's wagon was out of hearing range, Rev. Youngun sat Larry down on the porch steps. "I want you to promise me you won't go back up there. Those people have enough troubles without kids from town bothering them."

"But, Pa, they're meaner than Old Scrooge, treatin' those kids worse than pack mules."

"Aren't you exaggerating just a bit? Shouldn't you be acting your age?"

"No, Pa, they beat 'em bad. I seen 'em do it."

"Some children do need punishing. For discipline, like Mr. Robison said. Parents raise their children as they see fit."

"You gotta listen to me, Pa. They've got a girl locked up in the cold storage room who . . ." He stopped as another wracking cough shuddered through his father.

"What girl?"

"A girl named Darleda. And they cut her hair for no reason."

"And you know this girl?" Rev. Youngun gasped, trying to get his full breath back. "You're friends with her, is that it?"

"No, Pa, but I . . ."

"And you went to talk to her, is that it?"

"I'd never spoken to her before today. Honest. Her pa abandoned her and . . ."

"I'm not mad at you for talking with a girl, I just don't want you to go getting yourself in trouble. It's their property, and they have the right to tell you to keep off. And you promised."

Larry looked at his father, for the first time realizing that he, like other adults, really only listened to kids with half an ear. *They could be buryin' those kids in the well and he wouldn't believe me.* Larry knew he had tracked open a snake hole at the orphanage and had to go back there.

"Pa," he said, carefully choosing his words, not wanting to upset his sickly father. "You preached to me, to us, to the church, that fair is fair, that the law's the law, and that there's a difference 'tween right and wrong."

"Larry, I asked for your promise that you won't go back."

"I can't."

"Why?"

"'Cause you preached that the Lord hears the poor and don't despise the prisoners. Those kids are prisoners, Pa."

"They're orphans, and don't be quoting Psalms back on me."

"That woman's meaner than a water moccasin. You gotta do somethin'."

"You promise me that you'll stay off their land. And mean it. I'm giving you a second chance. You can't go through life breaking promises."

"If you promise to do somethin' to help them kids." Larry had never taken a stand against his father before. It was a telling moment in his life.

"I'll look into it. Just remember a young man is only as good as his word. Break that and you're breaking part of the fiber of your soul. Remember those words. I'll forgive you for going back this time, but that's it. Next time I'll have to punish you. Teach you some . . . discipline."

Larry didn't want to lie, didn't want to break his word, but all he could think about was going back to see Darleda Jackson. He drew no comfort from his father's promise to look into things. It seemed empty, hollow, like the promises adults made and broke without regard to how it affected a child's view of the world. Larry knew it was part of the commonsense smarts that kids seemed to pick up from the air.

If'n he don't do somethin' quick, then I'm goin' back—promise or no promise. He went inside and put Darleda's lock of hair inside a handkerchief and slipped it under his pillow.

32

Threshold

❖

Keeping to himself, Larry did his chores that night without speaking. Terry and Sherry tried to get him to smile and laugh when they got back from town, but he was too moody. With their father sick and Larry moping around, the other two kept as far away from the house as they could.

After dinner, Larry walked aimlessly through the fields, ending up on the edge of the Springers' property. He sat down on one of the rails of the Springers' fence, wondering what Darleda was doing. Maurice found him there, looking like the loneliest boy in the world.

"What's buggin' you?" Maurice asked.

"Nothin'."

"Nothin'? Ain't like you to mope around like this."

Larry looked at the man who'd been his confidant over the years and suddenly began to spill out his emotions. About Mr. Robison. About his father's not really listening to him. And most of all, about wanting to help Darleda. Maurice listened, knowing that the boy's heart had been pricked by Cupid's arrow.

"It's hard to know what you're supposed to do, ain't it, boy?"

"I know it," Larry said.

"You're still a boy, but your body's callin' out about girls and such."

"Can't talk to Pa 'bout this. He wouldn't understand."

Maurice belly laughed. "You think your pa weren't never a boy?"

"Can't see him as one."

"He was a boy just like you. Probably used to sit on a fence somewhere, havin' these same kinda worries that you don't need to be havin' at your age. How old are you now anyway?"

"Eleven."

"And you're sittin' out here all by your lonely?" A train whistled off in the dark distance. "Hear that?"

"Yup."

"Don't you ever lie awake at night and wonder where that ol' train be goin'? Wonder who's goin' where, chasin' dreams or facin' hurts?"

"Never thought 'bout it that way." Larry looked down. "What would you do, Mr. Springer, if you had my worries?"

"You're worryin' 'nough to take the warts off a fat toad. If'n it was me, why, I'd go climb a tall tree and let the wind wash my face. I'd be lookin' for blue sky to tell me that things will work out."

"Why?"

"'Cause you don't need to be growin' up so fast. Matter of fact, if you can keep from growin' up all your life, you'll be a happier person."

"Doesn't everybody grow up?"

"I ain't talkin' years. I'm talkin' in your mind. Don't let your young spirit get washed out with your too-small clothes."

"Pa says I should act my age."

Maurice chuckled. "Act your age, huh? Well, let me tell you somethin'. Folks be tellin' you that all your life 'cause they scared of kids."

"They are?"

"Sure 'nuff that's the truth. They scared 'cause they know they lost that spirit that lets a kid run through the grass, free as a bird, or skip down a sunny road like it's the most fun thing in the world." He put his hand on Larry's shoulder. "Once you lose it, it never comes back."

"It don't?"

"No, sir, that's why some fools drink so they can act like someone besides theyselves. And why womenfolk will fuss and fuss over a young girl's hair, 'cause it makes 'em remember back when they was that way, 'fore they got caught up in the ways of the world, tryin' to act the age that everyone told them they had to." He patted Larry's shoulder. "Boys want to be men, and men want to be boys. That's a fact of life."

Larry kicked the fence with the back of his shoe. "Guess that's just what growin' up means."

"Everyone grows up, but you don't got to get old. There's a big difference." He traced the lines under his eyes. "See these wrinkles? It don't matter if you're old, stooped and gray, you can still keep a free spirit in your heart like God intended."

"But how's that helpin' Darleda? Who's gonna help her?"

"I'm more worried 'bout you. She'll get adopted out, get a new family. But you're the one who's tryin' to grow up before you have to. Your pa's gonna do somethin' to help that girl. Don't you worry."

"You think she's all right?"

"Sure. She'll be fine. Orphanage is just a strict place, that's all."

Larry closed his eyes, unconvinced, knowing there were some things adults said that you listened to and some you took with a grain of salt. The season's last smell of Ozark honeysuckle tickled his nose, stirring his heart. Looking off toward where the orphanage was, he prayed that Darleda was okay.

33

Bad Dreams

❖

Sarah's world was crashing down around her. Nothing was going right. Mrs. Wilson was coming. It was only a matter of time until the Board learned the truth. Her fingers were locked around the Bible which was still closed. She looked at the daybed in her sewing room. Her eyelids were heavy, but she fought sleep as if it were the doors to an asylum.

Moonlight fought to get through the drape-shrouded room. The pain in her skull had a life of its own, like a caged beast slowly pushing apart the bars. Her stomach was knotted. She wanted to vomit, but all she could do was hold her forehead and wait, looking around vacantly with deep-set eyes that saw nothing.

It was like thick kudzu vines were squeezing off her brain. All she could see were the outlines of people, bad people from her past. No smiling faces, just frowns, screaming, scolding, mocking, laughing. Then the images turned into her own face and she saw the hair-trigger things she'd done and said to the children.

I'm going mad. I'm insane, she thought frantically. *They'll take me away. Put me back in a lunatic asylum. Never see the light of day.* Her lips were dry. It was the first sign of what was coming.

Boom, boom, boom.

She waited, swallowing breaths of air, trying to keep calm. Sour sweat half-moons formed under her arms. Insects hummed softly, but they were like a buzz saw in her mind.

Boom, boom, boom.

She clutched the table leg as the world seemed to shift on its axis. The Bible slipped off her lap. The drumbeat continued.

Boom, boom, boom, boom, boom.

Before, when she'd gotten off balance, it used to pass quickly. Now it was coming, one spell right after another. She wanted to scream, wanted to run from the room and drown herself to stop the pain, but she held on, gritting her teeth, grinding her jaws.

The spell passed, leaving her drenched with sweat. For a sane moment she thought about leaving the orphanage and going for help, but that was out of the question. She couldn't face being locked in another trouble room. Darleda represented the one last chance of goodness left in her life. The last chance to find the missing piece of her life and be cured.

Darleda's the key. She's the key to saving myself. I'll adopt her. Start a new life. Make her love me.

But the spiritual darkness surrounded her, blocking out the light she wanted to see. Her life seemed a rot of blasphemy, decay, and hurt children. What was done had been done. *I couldn't help myself. I did to them what had been done to me.*

"You gonna sleep in the sewing room?" John Robison asked through the door after knocking softly. He was ready to talk. Needed to talk. His own life of rough edges was coming unglued.

"Leave me alone," she grimaced, her voice raw, her lips trembling. She bit into her lip, making it bleed.

"Sarah, you know there's something wrong. It's time to hang up the fiddle. We gotta talk. I want to help you."

"No." Her eyes blinked insanely.

"Yes. Either talk to me or to the doctor. But we can't hide things any longer."

"John, don't you tell anyone anything. I can make it through the Board meeting. Then we'll talk about doctors. But don't tell anyone anything. Please."

He stood outside the door, shaking his head. "Never have told anyone . . . that's the problem," he muttered, trudging slowly off, praying for a dreamless sleep, not knowing the dark, evil thoughts that were raging in his wife's troubled mind.

She was crossing the point where no voice of reason could ever call her back. He heard her soft wail, a voice alone, without a connection to the world. Rising to go to her he stopped, wondering if it was something she needed to do.

Maybe a good cry will help her. Let her see the light.

She sounded so sad, so distraught, that it bit into his heart. But he believed that she was crying for forgiveness, which consoled him. He didn't know that she was standing on the edge, afraid to look down, knowing that she was falling, leaving everything behind, never to return.

The children heard her wailing and pulled their covers tight. As if that would protect them from the insanity.

Just a few miles away, Sherry sobbed in her sleep. She was terrified. The clammy air was suffocating. The Dark Hats from the orphanage were coming for her. Alone in her dark room, lost in a far-off world of disjointed sleep, she fought to save herself. The rain pounding on the tin roof of her bedroom became the hoofbeats of demons coming to get her in her dream.

Sherry screamed until her throat was so raspy and raw that only silent screams escaped. "Sherry, wake up, wake up," her father said, struggling to hold her in his arms, but the sickness had sapped most of his strength. "Your heart's beating like a team of horses."

She blinked, struggled fiercely, then went limp, exhausted from the chase. "The Dark Hats had me. They had me, Pa."

Her body relaxed in his arms. "You're all right. It was just a dream. Just a bad dream."

"Don't let the Dark Hats get me, Pa."

"I won't. I'll always be here to protect you." Rev. Youngun rocked his daughter back to sleep.

Larry poked a sleepy head into the room. "She all right, Pa?"

"Just fine, just fine. She had a nightmare."

"About the Dark Hats?" Larry asked.

Rev. Youngun nodded. "Who are the Dark Hats?" he asked, as he laid Sherry back down.

"The Robisons. They wear those funny-looking black hats."

Sherry's worried about being taken to the orphanage, Rev. Youngun thought. *She's worried that I'm going to die. Like Norma.* His body was suddenly racked by a coughing spasm that forced him to sit back down.

34

The Hint

❖

The lead story in the *Monitor* the next morning was about what Dr. George and Henry Mead had seen. It confirmed what all the backyard fence gossips had been whispering about.

Missouri Mud Monster Eats Dog!
Five Hundred Dollar Reward Offered!

Baying hounds and rifle fire could be heard in all directions. Every farm boy for twenty miles around had arrived to try for Tippy's reward. Sheriff Peterson could do nothing except hope that they didn't shoot themselves. It was bad enough that his phone line was burning up with reports of cows, horses, and dogs being shot in the frenzy.

While no one was sure exactly what they were tracking, every animal track was worth following. Only two seasoned hunters had sought out Mead and asked him enough questions to get themselves on target. Though it was barely dawn, the hounds were furious, barking madly, frothing at the mouth. Rapid-fire howling filled the air throughout the area. The predawn hunt had turned into a rout as the hunters followed the tracks deep into the woods. The sun was a burnished ball inching upward. The two hunters ran behind the dogs, thinking only about the five-hundred-dollar reward from Tippy. Their rundown boot heels attested to their need for the money.

Up ahead, the hounds had treed the cougar who was snarling, its open mouth showing sharp, huge fangs. Its green eyes were glaring like it was ready to cut the dogs into shreds with its claws. The dogs were so upset that the bristles on their backs were straight up. They bit at the tree limbs, eating chunks of bark. When they heard the hunters approaching, their howls raised in volume until the pack of six sounded like a dozen demented dogs howling to beat the band.

"What the heck's up there?" the burly hunter with close-set eyes wondered.

"Seems like we got ourselves a reward comin'," his older, gray-haired companion said, his fleshy liver-spotted hands knuckle-white gripped around his rifle. Upper teeth gnawed lightly at his split lower lip.

"Can you get a shot?" the other hunter asked in a wire-tight voice.

"Maybe from that fallen log over there." The older man stepped through the brush, breathing hard. They'd covered five miles in the past hour. He lowered his head to catch a breath, worried for a moment that he might faint. "Pard, it sounds like a cat to me," he said, aiming up into the tree, the sunlight from the bleached sky directly in his eyes.

Visions of demons were the unspoken thoughts that bonded both men with fear. "Mead said this monster was half cat," the big man said.

"Not by a jugful here. I think it's all cat. I think we treed ourselves a big, ornery cougar," said the man with gray hair.

"Gonna be a tough cat to skin if you ask me."

Things happened fast. Both men tried to get a shot, but the tree was shaking under the weight of the cat. Overwhelmed by fear, jagged breaths, howling and frenzied dogs, it was hard to concentrate. The thought in both men's minds was that this was the shape-changing monster.

The old cougar growled, swinging its paws, wishing it could claw one of the dogs up into the tree. As the hunters fired, it leaped, legs spread like an eagle, and landed in the brush and rolled down the rocks.

"Missed!" the burly hunter shouted.

"Come on!"

The dogs took off on the cougar's heels. The cougar landed hard but quickly regained its footing, racing off at full speed through the ravine.

35

Red Eyes

❖

Eulla Mae went about her kitchen business, putting away the supplies they'd brought from town while the sweet potato pies cooked in the oven. She straightened out the rag rug and closed up the Arbuckle's coffee can. Normally, the late afternoon noises of the Ozarks, which were always alive with God's life, were like a soothing balm to her soul, but with all the hunters blasting up the hills, it was all she could do to ignore it.

Checking on the pies one more time, she notched another vent in the top crust of each, then closed the heavy oven door. It had taken a while to boil their home-grown sweet potatoes, but the skin had fallen right off and she'd mashed them together with heaps of butter, three eggs, a teaspoon of vanilla, grated nutmeg, and three cups of sweet brown sugar.

"Gonna make my man a treat he deserves," she said. Maurice had eaten almost the whole pie himself the night before and asked her to make more.

The pies would be ready in a few minutes, so she busied herself in the pantry, straightening the molasses, dried apples, cornmeal, and the canned oysters that they'd never opened. She and Maurice had come a long way from the one-room log cabin they'd first started in, back when Maurice married her when she was just fifteen, promising her the world come better or worse. Now she felt like they'd walked a million miles in each other's shoes.

A blue jay landed on the windowpane, tap-tapping away. "No more food today. You ate all that bread too quick." She laughed, looking out at the empty feeder.

She could tell by the aroma that the pies were ready, so she carefully lifted them from the oven, using the thick towels to keep from burning her fingers. Then she set them on the front porch to cool off and opened the jar of herb sun tea which she was brewing up for Rev. Youngun. *Gotta get that man healthy again. Lord knows he's got enough burdens without losin' his health.*

Lifting her cotton dress to keep it from catching on the table leg, she came back through the door. Outside, the world was alive with animal chatter, crickets, and the answers that the penned-up barn animals sent out to their wild cousins. It made her think of the children she wished she could have had, but God had not given her any children. Now, on the shady side of forty, she'd resigned herself to a life of growing old, alone with Maurice.

Then a shiver went up her arms. There wasn't a sound to be heard outside. Not a chirp. Even the croaking bullfrogs had gone silent. Deathly silent. Eulla Mae heard a scraping at the window and turned. Staring back at her were huge eyes. Intense. Frightening. "Oh dear," she whispered, falling back into the corner chair. The smell of rotten eggs and moldy featherbeds seemed to seep through the walls, assaulting her nose.

Whatever was at the window moved its massive hand up and down. Not waving. Not calling her out. Just up and down, pushing at the glass, trying to get in.

"Go on, get back to where you came from!" she screamed, jumping to her feet. There wasn't a moment to lose. Eulla Mae ran into the kitchen and grabbed her broom, hitting it against the front door.

The creature jumped back and forth on the porch, then pushed and pounded against the door. Eulla Mae put her weight against it, turning the key to lock it, and prayed the hinges would hold. The creature grunted then began hooting. She felt a double thick line of goose bumps go up her back as all the childhood fears of nightmarish creatures who stalked the woods, lurking in the undergrowth, came back.

Then it was gone. And it had eaten one of Maurice's pies.

36

Billy Goat Man

❖

The small man sat in the box-sized wagon, scanning the hills, looking for the lost chimpanzee named Sweet. The wagon wasn't much more than a converted dog cart, but all the gewgaws and colorful circus trimmings made it a real eye-catcher. He cleared his throat, shooting off a louie, sick of seeing the miles of zigzag split rail fences which looked like they'd been put up by drunks and blind men.

Farmers just stopped and stared as his wagon clip-clopped by. One old boy had come running out in his long johns with a shotgun and chased him away, calling him a devil, when all Billy had wanted to do was rest. No one in Wright County had ever seen a team of goats pulling a wagon, let alone a goat wagon being driven by a dwarf dressed in goatskins that he'd dressed, cut, and stitched himself. The gimmick worked in the circus, and Billy Goat credited borrowing the custom from Daniel Defoe's *Robinson Crusoe,* character for his act, which pleased parents and children alike. It had been years since he'd been called William Carlin, his birth name. To the world he was just Billy or Billy Goat Man. The circus star.

He was tuckered out from driving every trace, back road, and mud path that he could find, ending up at log houses, talking to dummies holding lard-oil lamps, who thought he was from another world.

"I've seen some bumpkins before, but these rubes take the cake. Just 'cause they ain't never seen a forty-goat team wagon before in their sorry lives."

A dog followed after him howling at the goat team. "Sweet's got to be here someplace," he said, cracking the small whip over the goats that were pulling him toward Mansfield. He'd begun to think that he might be wasting his time. All he had seen were lazy dogs, fat cows, varmints, snakes, and smoke curling from dozens of stovepiped, tar-papered shacks hidden for good reason by the trees.

"Can't imagine bein' a farmer," he frowned, thinking his life with the circus was far better than spending his time looking up the rear end of a mule pulling a plow.

He was hungry for something—anything—but he hadn't eaten a good meal since he started his search. Only a handful of wild hazelnuts which he could have done without. His stomach whinnied like a horse crying out for beef dodgers and apple dumplings, which he knew was the meal he was missing back at the circus feeding car.

Ever since the chimpanzee had gotten loose from the traveling circus show in the next county over, Billy Goat Man had taken a leave from W. W. Cole's New Colossal Show to try and catch him. Now he was wondering if he was wasting his time and moaned about his druthers. "Wish I had a warm bed. Hot food. Shoulda stayed with the circus train." He heard make-believe calliope music in his mind.

To anyone else it would have seemed dangerous. Sweet, whom they billed as "The Killer Ape from the Congo," was smaller than a human but could easily lift more than a six-foot man could. Billy had seen him toss drunks against the wall when they tried to hurt him. Billy Goat Man had befriended the ape in small ways. Bringing him fresh fruit and vegetables, and occasionally fresh bird eggs, the dwarf man who dressed in goatskins had bonded with the ape. "I gotta find him. I need Cole's reward real bad."

Clicking the reins, the tiny driver watched the woods, listening for Sweet's familiar hooting. In his carry sack was a load of sweet potatoes which Billy knew that the chimp craved. It was his favorite food. That was why he figured he could find Sweet and bring him back to the circus before he hurt someone unintentionally. Or someone killed him. Billy knew how scared the hill people were of the caged chimp and could only imagine what they'd do if he tried to get into their house when he was hungry.

W. W. Cole's New Colossal Show circus was a three-ring circus with dog-and-pony shows that crisscrossed the continent entertaining the public. Most Americans had never been to a zoo, and the big animals of Africa were still unknown. P. T. Barnum had brought an elephant and other animals to New York, but the people of the Ozarks had never seen a chimpanzee before. Sweet was quite a draw because he looked like a hairy human that did tricks.

Sweet did look a lot like a person. With no tail, hairless hands and face, and fingernails and toenails instead of claws or hooves, he could carry his food and walk upright when he wanted to. With his long arms, he could swing through the branches as well as pick up a grape with his precision grip.

When the train car broke down, Sweet was on his way to a show in Sikeston. The chimp bounced around, then found his cage burst open. Freedom. He'd never been on his own. Raised in captivity, the ape knew only the world from behind cage bars. So he had run off into the hills, leaving the circus behind.

Billy guided his goat team up the Springers' curved road into their farm. He needed to see if anyone had seen the ape, and it was well past dinner and Billy was mighty hungry.

"What the heck is that?" Terry asked, watching the strange looking little wagon approach. He and Sherry had come over to pester the Springers after finishing their afternoon chores.

Maurice had just gotten Eulla Mae calmed down and didn't need any more surprises in his life. "Looks like somethin' that escaped from *Alice in Wonderland*," he said.

"Man, would I like to have that thing," Terry said, imagining himself racing into town behind a forty-goat team. "That's some piece of work."

"Land sakes, what would you do with it?" Eulla Mae asked.

"Just ride around, eatin' candy, makin' people pay for a ride in my goat mobile." Terry watched the unusual contraption clippity-clop closer, determined that he'd figure a way to wangle a ride.

Billy Goat pulled up to a stop in front of the porch. "Excuse me folks, I was passin' through and . . ."

Terry couldn't help interrupting him. "Would you take me 'fore a ride in that thing?"

Billy grinned. He knew how children loved his wagon. "Maybe sometime, son."

Terry frowned. "Maybe sometime" was adult language for "not now" or "be quiet." "Why are you dressed like a goat?"

"Son, I always dress this way."

"Why? Do the goats like pullin' their cousins wrapped 'round you like some kind of wild man?"

"It's just part of my act for the circus. Folks call me Billy Goat Man."

"Do you baa like a goat and eat cans too?" Terry asked. Maurice gave him the "hush" look, but Terry ignored him. "And which one of those skins was Billy? Don't look like your mama born you to eat cans."

Maurice gave him a shove. "Don't pay him no heed," he said apologetically.

"Yeah," Sherry said, "my brother's a squirrel."

Billy ignored Terry and looked directly at Maurice. "I'm looking for a creature who might . . ."

"A big one. Kind of hairy. Walks on his hind legs?"

That got Billy's interest. "You seen him?"

"He was here," Eulla Mae said.

"And we saw him up on the road yesterday," Sherry added.

"And he stinks like a dead fish at high noon." Terry grinned.

"Which way did he go?"

"Why you lookin' for a wild stink bug?" Terry asked. *Man would I like to ride off in that wagon,* he thought.

"Chimp, son, it's a chimpanzee," Billy explained.

"What's a champ-zee?" Sherry asked.

"It's like a big monkey."

"Ain't never seen a monkey," Sherry shrugged.

Billy told them a little about chimpanzees and what they looked like.

"Didn't look like no ape to me that we saw," Maurice said, shaking his head. "If'n I coulda gotten a clear shot, I'd have me a fur rug come morning."

"Did you shoot it?" Billy gasped.

"Naw, it ran away 'fore I could shoot its head off."

"Thank God," Billy said.

"You ought to thank me," Terry said. "We was gonna shoot it, but I knew it had a goat daddy somewhere, so I grabbed Mr. Springer's arm and . . ."

"Look," Billy said impatiently, "I need to find him and bring him back. He wouldn't hurt a flea."

Maurice looked the little man up and down. "You think you're gonna go rompin' through the woods, dressed like a fool, guidin' a team of can-eaters an' catch you an ape?"

"It knows me."

"What's its name?" Sherry asked.

"Sweet Potato."

Eulla Mae made a face. "Sweet Potato? Why that thing done ate my sweet potato pie that I'd baked for Maurice."

Billy grinned. "He loves sweet potato pie. I used to get the cooks to make him one after each show."

"What kinda show?" Terry asked.

"Circus. He's one of the stars of the Cole Circus. Sweet is called the Killer Ape from the Congo and . . ." Billy pulled out a handbill advertising Sweet's act, with a drawing of the chimp.

"Killer ape," Eulla Mae whispered, covering her mouth.

"That's just his stage name. He's really harmless. He likes to play, ride a bike, and . . ."

Sherry cocked her head. "Ride a bike?"

"Sure, and Sweet does other tricks. He's curious like a kid. Heck, he's been raised all his life in a cage and doesn't know a lick about the woods. I just need to find him and take him back to the circus where he'll be safe."

Maurice frowned. "Slim chance of that. The boys 'round here are already out huntin' in packs, drinkin' like no get-out, wantin' to be the one that bags the ape so's they can have a lifetime of bar brags."

"I don't get a reward if he's dead," Billy Goat said—and then winced. Once these people knew Cole had offered a reward, they'd want to find Sweet themselves.

"Reward? What kind of reward?" Terry asked.

Maurice cautioned Terry. "Now don't you be thinkin' 'bout headin' off into the woods, huntin' with your little stick rifle."

"I could borrow yours." *And that wagon,* Terry thought, imagining himself riding through the woods, cracking the whip, carrying Maurice's shotgun.

"No, I've heard that chimps eat small kids like they was breakfast toast with jelly," Maurice said.

"No, Sweet's not like that," Billy protested. "He's nice if you're nice to him. Why, he'll even kiss you if you give him another pie."

"No thanks. What else does this thing eat?" Maurice asked. "Pork shoulder barbecue? Maybe a slab or two of spareribs? Or how 'bout some mashed taters with thick gravy?"

"I like all that," Terry nodded, rubbing his tummy.

"I just don't want anything to happen to Sweet Potato, that's all," Billy said.

Maurice snapped his fingers. "You lookee here. You want your reward money, but I'm worried about protectin' these kids. I saw that thing. It stank worse'n a sunny day road kill and had teeth that would scare a dentist."

"But he's harmless. All he likes to eat is fruit, leaves, seeds, and flowers. Give him some ants and honey, maybe even a few caterpillars, and he'll hoot in happiness."

"How much is the ree-ward?" Terry asked.

"Five hundred dollars."

Terry was momentarily speechless. That was all the money in the world. "And you say this chimp likes sweet potatoes?"

"Loves 'em."

Sherry was curious. "Why does your monkey stink so bad?"

"Don't know. Dirty I guess."

"You better be holdin' your nose if you find him, 'cause he stinks worse than my friend Pin Worm," Terry grinned. "Say, can I ride in your goat wagon?"

"If you help me find Sweet, I'll let you take her for a spin."

Eulla Mae put her foot down. "Don't be tellin' this boy that. Next thing you know he'll be ridin' off to trouble."

"But I wanna," Terry protested.

"No," Maurice said. He looked at Billy. "Don't be lettin' ol' Red here try and talk you into somethin'. This kid could talk the horns off your billy goats if you gave him half a chance."

Billy ruffled Terry's hair. "Sorry, kid." The goats began baaing. "Could you folks spare some water for the animals?"

Eulla Mae wiped her hands on her apron. "Maurice, you take those goats to the barn. Mr. Billy, are you hungry?"

"Powerful hungry." The little man grinned.

"Come on in then." She went into the kitchen and brought out a pitcher of water, a basin, and soap for Billy to wash up.

Terry started down the steps. "I'll take your goats to the barn."

Maurice grabbed him by the collar. "Don't you be gettin' in and ridin' off in that thing."

"Never in a million years."

"Don't care 'bout a million years and all your book talk. Just don't you be squirrelin' off, takin' this goat wagon and doin' no good."

"You got my word on it."

"I can take no comfort in that." Maurice sighed, shaking his head and pushed the boy playfully forward.

Terry looked at the wagon, knowing that he could find the chimp if he had a goat wagon to drive. He'd had a bellyful of adults and their rules. He was up to his ears with don'ts and warnings.

Walking to the front of the goat line, Terry pulled them forward. *Boy's gotta do what he wants to do,* he reasoned. "Come on, can-eaters. March."

37

Cat and Mouse

❖

Sweet didn't want to hurt anybody. All he wanted to do was have somebody feed him like they did at the circus. Like the man who smelled like goats did. Sniffing his own matted coat, the sweet scent of Eulla Mae's pie came through. Sweet wanted more. If he could only remember where that house was.

Life was different out here from in his cage. The woods were alive. After the hunters had killed his mother in Africa, he was locked in a wooden crate and shipped to America with other baby chimps. Of the thirty that had been sent, Sweet was the only one that had survived. He had grown up being fed by the humans who forced him to do the tricks in front of the crowds. But sometimes, when it was dark, he could remember hanging on to his mother, drinking her milk, sharing her nest, learning from her about the forest. Sweet wasn't sure where that place was, only that he'd fallen from the trees when his mother had screamed out, dropping him as the bullet ripped through her brain.

The dogs were on his mind now. He'd seen the pack of wild scavenger dogs attack the pig, ripping it apart in a frenzy. The pig had squealed and fought until the end. The dogs had tracked his scent all night, not knowing that they'd chased the pig under the tall tree where the chimp had built a platform mattress of broken, leafy branches near the top of the tree. Holding on to the branches, Sweet hoped that the dogs couldn't climb trees.

Sweet ran through the woods, hesitated at the sunlit field that seemed to stretch forever, then set out across it, trying to remember where the pie house was. Through the grasses and wildflowers, jumping over the fallen juniper tree, bouncing off the side of the lone rock, Sweet frolicked, enjoying the freedom.

For a moment he was free. Free of the dogs chasing him. Free of the humans shooting at him. In the middle of the field, the ape stopped to pick at the prairie roses and the Indian paintbrush flowers, still blooming late in the year.

Then he froze, feeling the danger in the air. Somewhere, something, an animal, was watching, waiting, wanting to attack. Sweet spun around on all fours, making soft, frightened sounds. It was the cougar. He could smell it. There, back at the edge of the tree line he'd just left stood the cougar. Sweet watched it prowl. The cougar pranced back and forth, hesitating, as if it, too, was unsure what to do.

The strange-looking ape had caught the cougar's attention. The cat didn't know if it was a smelly human or a big dog. It stalked through the tall grass, emerging to roar from the top of the boulder. Leaping onto the same fallen tree that Sweet had crossed, it lifted up its leg, marking the tree as its territory. Yowling loudly, the cougar paced back and forth to begin its deadly came of cat and mouse. The tree creaked and groaned under the cougar's weight. A thick branch broke, and the cat tumbled to the ground, once again out of sight in the brush.

Sweet jumped up and down, not knowing which way to run. He could smell blood on the cat. Fresh-kill blood. Instinct told the ape that this hunter would attack. He listened in the wind, trying to get a sense of direction of where the cat was from the soft whine of the breeze that swept up and over the field. Sweet spun around and around, not knowing which way to flee. Then, not twenty feet away, he heard a low, rumbling growl. The cat charged and leaped. Sweet fell and rolled behind a rock, then bounded off on all fours. The wind seemed to roar in his ears, blocking out his senses, but it was just the fear and need to escape that had panicked him.

At the far edge of the field, the cougar's claws grabbed at the back of the chimp's neck, pulling at his fur, trying to kill him. Blood streamed down his neck, catching in the ape's coat. Then the cougar pulled the chimp down, both rolling and crashing into the trees. They rocked back and forth, the air filled with animal screams of blood lust and fear. A claw snagged on Sweet's back, opening another gash. The chimp cried out to stave off the death throes. He could feel the burning claws digging into his neck, squeezing the life out of him. Desperate, the ape reached back, desperately trying to pull the lion off, then spun in a circle, crashing into a pine and jarring the cat loose.

The cougar let loose a bloodcurdling roar as it tried to get its balance after the jarring blow. Howling in pain, the cat's muscles quivered, wanting to kill. It whirled around, disoriented, clawing at the air like a death wind. Sweet crawled through the dead leaves trying to get away. He was bleeding and needed to get to safety. To hide. To find a creek to wash his wounds. There was no time. All he could do was keep crawling, keep moving. He had to get away from the claws.

The cat watched Sweet struggle down the hill and disappear into the dark woods. There was other, easier game to get. Like cows and sheep. Maybe even children. The old mountain lion lumbered back across the open field following the smell of sheep in the air.

38

Racing Goats

❖

Sherry listened as the funny-looking circus man ate supper and told tales taller than himself. Eulla Mae served up ham on bread with sides of beans, rice, corn bread, dried green beans, and sorghum. Billy Goat Man had the worst table manners any of them had ever seen, eating with his fingers, spilling the rice, sopping up the gravy with the crust. After he wolfed his food down, he sat back and belched.

"That was sure good."

Eulla Mae was dumbfounded. "Glad you liked it."

"I'll take some coffee if you're offering."

A funny smell tickled Sherry's nose. At first she thought it was from the goatskins, but as she moved closer to the little man, she knew where it came from.

Sniffing at the man's head, she asked, "How come your hair smells sweet and sour?"

"'Cause I keeps it clean the right way," he said awkwardly, not used to being around kids.

"With what?"

"Why, with New England rum. Keeps it clean and free of lice and mites."

Sherry got on her tiptoes and sniffed again. "Don't your hair get drunk?"

"Hair get drunk? That's the dumbest thing I ever heard," Billy said.

"Sounds dumb to pour rum on your head. Just a few inches from your mouth. What happens if you slip and you wash your tongue instead?"

"Leave the man be," Eulla Mae said. She wanted to hear more gossip about the hootchy-kootchy woman and the strong man in the circus.
"How come you don't get a real car?" Sherry asked.
"Don't need one. Got the only goat wagon in the world."

While the adults sat and gossiped on the back steps, Terry took the reins of the lead goat and walked them back to the barn. How he was going to water forty goats didn't matter; all he wanted to do was get the wagon behind the house.

Looking around to make sure no one was looking, Terry climbed into the mini-wagon and stood up like he was driving a chariot. In his mind he was racing down the dark streets of St. Louis, green glass jar headlights filled with lightning bugs, a mouth full of gumdrops, not a care in the world.

"You can-eaters ready to race?" he called out. The goats baaed back, smelling the water from the trough.

"Well, if'n you want water, you gotta walk to it. Now mush." It was the only word he could think of to call out to them.

The goats lurched forward, knocking Terry backward. He caught his balance and cracked the whip. "Mush, head on out, giddiyap, move your can-eatin' behinds."

Half the goats turned around baaing, wondering who Terry was. "Lookee here, I'm the new goat skinner 'round these parts so move if you know what's good for you." And move they did.

Maurice looked up just as the goat wagon came flying around the side of the house. "What the heck?" he exclaimed.

Terry was holdin' on for dear life, the forty goats moving like a centipede that had drunk a hundred cups of coffee. "Whoa, Nelly bell, slow down, dig a hole, and stop!"

"Terry, bring that thing back here!" Maurice called out through the window.

Dangit the dog came flying after them, howling, scaring the goats half to death. The goats held to a tight circle around the house, dog chasing, Maurice screaming, Billy jumping up and down, Eulla Mae closing her eyes, and Sherry jealous that Terry was having all the fun.

"Get outta my wagon!" Billy screamed.
"Tell the goats to stop!" Terry screamed back.

Finally, Maurice ran out and grabbed the back of the wagon, dragging it to a halt. "What you do a fool thing like that for?" he asked Terry.

Terry saw Billy Goat Man coming up fast, so he had to think of a good one. "There was this big rattler near the waterin' trough that tried to bite the goats. I fought the thing with a stick, and then the goats started runnin' and not wantin' them to hurt themselves, and all I could do was try to stop them."

"That was a brave thing to do," Billy said.

Maurice knew better but didn't say anything, just giving Terry the eye that he knew better.

Ten minutes later Billy Goat Man rode off toward town to see if anyone else had seen the ape.

Terry looked at Sherry. "We need a goat wagon. Man, was that fun."

Maurice laughed. "We better go catch us that rattler."

"I drove it off. There's nothin' to worry 'bout," Terry grinned. He watched Billy crack the whip as he drove away. "That's the life for me."

"Would you go 'round dressed like that?" Eulla Mae asked.

"For money? Sure. And I'd take Sherry along as my sidekick. I'd call her Cockroach Girl."

Sherry screamed and chased Terry off the porch.

Eulla Mae sat down next to her husband. "That ape I saw didn't look friendly to me."

"Don't think no one's gonna be collectin' the circus reward on that thing. Anyway, paper says Tippy's offering a reward for killin' the thing. But I didn't have the heart to tell the goat man. Trophy kills like that don't come 'round but once in an Ozark lifetime."

He shouted to Sherry to come help feed the livestock. "And Terry, you come over here and sweep the steps."

"Can't, gotta go bad," he fibbed, heading off to the privy. Terry stopped to watch Billy go over the hill. *I'm gonna drive that thing myself again. There's got to be a way for me to get that wagon and take off.*

Orphaned Fawns

❖

Little Jim hobbled through the late afternoon woods that bordered the orphanage property. He was supposed to be walking the fence, checking for breaks, but he wanted to check on the two orphaned fawns that he'd found after the hunters had killed their mother.

It had been hard keeping them a secret, but he'd only told Darleda. Little Jim knew that if Mrs. Robison found out about the milk he was sneaking out to feed them and the kitchen food he'd stolen, something worse than the trouble room would happen to him.

The two deer pranced lively in the corral of the old barn. Their spotted coats were beautiful—the most beautiful sight he'd ever seen. And they were his pets to love.

Inside the pen, they snuggled close against him, still small but no longer the weak, dying creatures he'd found. They needed their mother's milk, but he'd done the best he could. Just keeping them alive was a miracle in itself, what with all the wild dogs and wolves around. They cried out to be fed and Little Jim laughed. "I'm not your mother, hold on," he giggled, pulling his shirttail from the larger one's mouth.

They had already eaten all the leaves that hung low over the pen, so Little Jim knew that he would soon have to release them. Gathering an armful of grass, leaves, and twigs, he made a pile in the corner of the pen.

Then he heard a scratching at the back of the barn. Turning around slowly, expecting to see Darleda smiling at him, he was instead confronted by a smelly creature unlike anything he'd ever seen.

"Mud Monster," was all Little Jim could manage to croak out, hoping he wouldn't wet his pants in fear.

The creature moved forward, hooting quietly. Picking up a piece of bread, the creature tossed it up and down in his hands, then tossed it to Little Jim. But the boy was too scared to catch it. Little Jim didn't run—he couldn't have run with his bad leg—so he stood in place watching the creature climb over the makeshift gate.

"Don't hurt my deer," he pleaded quietly, pushing the two fawns behind him. The creature cocked his head, wondering why the boy hadn't run away like the other humans. Then he saw more bread slices in Little Jim's carry sack and grabbed them and ran off hooting. All Little Jim could do was watch and pray that the creature didn't come back hungry for anything else.

Little Jim whispered to Darleda over the dishes later that night about what he'd seen at the fawn's pen. "It was big. Smelled bad too."

"You think it was that Mud Monster Mr. Mead was talking about?" Darleda asked.

"Couldn't be nothin' else. I was afraid he was gonna eat me or the fawns, but he just ate the ol' stale bread and then took off."

"Just like that?"

"Just like that," Little Jim nodded.

Darleda thought for a moment. "Maybe later you could draw me a picture of it."

Mrs. Robison looked around the corner. "What are you talking about? Don't you know the rules? You are to be silent while you do your chores."

"Sorry, Mrs. Robison," Little Jim said.

"We were just talking about Adoption Day, that's all," Darleda said, hoping this confrontation would quickly end.

"No talking," Mrs. Robison said. "Remember that."

When the coast was clear, Little Jim drew what he remembered. "And its hair was dark, thick, like a brush."

"Those look like hands," she exclaimed, pointing to the front paws.

"I know. Thing walked upright, kinda hunched over like an old man. Had four hands."

"Four hands?"

Jim nodded. Darleda studied the picture. "I've seen pictures in the magazines that show apes. I think they live in Africa."

"You got a picture of this thing?"

"In the pantry, behind the flour sacks. Come on."

Little Jim followed behind. "Why'd you hide it in here?"

"'Cause Mrs. Robison don't want us to have anything like this. Only the *McGuffey Readers*. You know her rules—no contact with the world."

She flipped through the magazine then stopped. "Did it look like this?" she asked, pointing to a shaggy ape.

"That's it!" Little Jim gasped. "But what's it doing over here? Missouri's a long way from Africa."

"You sure that's what you saw?" Darleda asked.

"Sure as rain."

Darleda gave him the eye. "It's not rainin'."

"That's what I saw. A chim-pan-zee out there in the fawn's pen."

Bath Time

❖

Sherry finished up her chores, then headed out to the barn to feed the pigs. Terry was still hiding in the privy so she knew he wouldn't be jumping out, trying to scare her. Dumping half the pail of table scraps into the pen, she stopped and sniffed the air. She smelled something.

The ape had crept down toward the house, seeking food. He didn't want to hurt the little girl; as a matter of fact, the chimp wanted to play with her. Holding out his hand, he made soft hooting sounds.

Sherry didn't move. She knew something was behind her. "Who's there?"

The chimp hooted back.

"Is that you, Terry?" she asked anxiously.

No answer, just hoots.

"Thought you were hiding in the privy."

Silence. Finally, mustering all the courage she had in the world, Sherry inched around with her eyes closed.

The chimp cocked his head, and moved closer.

Sherry sniffed the air. "Whatever you are, you sure need a bath."

Sweet leaned forward and kissed Sherry on the cheek. She opened her eyes, wanting to scream, but her voice was frozen. She'd never seen an ape, not even a picture of one. All she knew was that she was alone with this thing that looked kind of like a hairy person. In her mind she was thinking of the Mud Monster, forgetting what the Billy Goat Man had told them.

"Please don't eat me, Mr. Mud Monster."

The chimp hooted softly, pointing to the scraps in the bucket.

"I don't want to die," Sherry moaned.

Sweet jumped up and down, pointing his finger at the bucket.

"Are you hungry?" she managed to croak out.

Sweet hooted, holding out his hand. Sherry reached into the bucket and took out a piece of apple. "Here," she said, holding it out.

The chimp took the apple core between his thumb and fingers and held it up to his mouth. Then it disappeared down his throat.

"Want more?" she asked, holding out the bucket.

Sweet took it from her hand and poured out the remains. He held up a piece of soggy bread to her.

"No thanks," she giggled. The chimp clapped his hands, making a series of funny faces.

"You're not a monster, are you?"

Sweet leaned over and smooched her again. Then he heard the baying dogs and started hooting loudly.

"Those dogs smell you a mile away," Sherry said. Sweet spun around, clapping and hooting. "You stink skunk bad," she said. She pointed to the water trough. "If you stand over here, I'll scrub you with cleanin' oil till the stink comes off."

Sherry took the scrub brush off the wall and motioned for the chimp to come over. Sweet hesitated, then moved closer to Sherry. He remembered how they had washed him back at the circus and stood patiently.

"That's good. Now stand right there and I'll get you smellin' good." Without a worry, she dipped the brush into the trough, poured cleaning oil onto the bristles, then scrubbed away. Sweet moved like it was tickling him, making funny faces. Sherry giggled as she scrubbed, wondering why everyone had been so afraid of this strange-looking creature.

When she was finished, she said, "You stay here. I'm gonna get my brother."

But the ape heard the baying dogs heading back toward the Youn-guns' and ran back into the woods. When Sherry returned with Terry, the ape was gone and Terry was more than skeptical.

"But he was here," Sherry protested. "Smelled real bad and . . ."

Terry interrupted her. "Don't be blamin' some make-believe ape 'cause you let a bunny."

"I did not! He was here. And I washed him."

"Uh-huh. You're standin' here, straight-faced, tellin' me that you and a stinky ape took a bath together like it was Saturday night at the zoo?"

"I didn't take a bath. I washed him."

Terry whistled. "You're a bald-faced fibber."

"Am not."

"You just got the sweets for that Billy Goat Man, don'tcha'?" Terry teased.

"No. I'm tellin' the truth."

"Don't be tellin' anyone that you're seein' apes. They'll think you're loony," he advised.

"But I did too see it," Sherry repeated in frustration.

"You were dreamin' again."

"Was not."

"You go around sayin' you gave a bath to an ape, and they'll think you got a broken cuckoo clock for a head."

"But I did see it. I did."

"Yeah, and I saw the man in the moon," Terry said, fluttering his lips.

"Mr. Springer will believe me."

"That's what you think. But when you go to sleep, he'll call the nuthouse and book you a lifetime room."

"He would?" Sherry asked.

"Yeah. Put you in with a toe-eatin' fruitcake."

"A what?"

"One of them loony birds that eat toes. You'd have to wear wooden feet and hobble 'round on crutches." Terry shook his head. "I think maybe I should tell him. Warn him that you've cracked your egg head."

Suddenly Sherry had second thoughts. "No, don't."

"You got any candy?"

She nodded. "Two gumdrops in my pocket."

"Give me one and I won't blab."

A moment later Terry skipped out of the barn, happy that he'd pulled another fast one.

Bad Scene

❖

Billy Goat Man arrived in Mansfield after dusk. He was huffed, hot, and tired. It had been a powerfully hot and frustrating day of nothing. Everybody he spoke to thought he was pulling a humbug on them with a hoax about the chimp being friendly. They slapped his back, telling him he could tell a good hooter of a tale.

"I wasn't tryin' to honey-fuggle any of 'em," he grumbled to himself.

For hours he'd driven his goat wagon through the hills but hadn't seen the chimp. He had wanted to find Sweet before word got out, but he was already too late to stop the hunters who had grabbed their guns to earn the reward.

He stopped into the saloon where a liquor-primed crowd was ready to let things rip. Billy wasn't up to listening to fiddle songs, so he took a stool at the bar and plunked down his money.

"Corn whiskey," he ordered.

"Comin' right up."

The rambunctious crowd was loud, boisterous, and ready to get rowdy. There were poker and faro tables going full tilt. Farm boys were dropping half dollars in a fast-moving chuck-a-luck dice game in the corner.

The food was pretty much picked over. The corn dodgers were past history, and there weren't enough chicken gizzards to make an old bird whole. Half eaten plates of mock oysters were spilled over the bar. Billy hated the fried-in-oil mixture of corn, eggs, butter, and flour that they tried to pass for the real thing. But he did try the pretzels and potato chips which were just a little soggy.

Billy kept to himself, talking with the bartender who was scrubbing beer mugs in hot, soapy water. Before he could even order a pickled egg, he saw the crudely drawn reward poster.

"What's that?"

"That, my little friend, is what all the shootin's 'bout." He told Billy about Tippy's reward. "Every jackleg farmer for a hundred miles be killin' anythin' that walks, crawls, or flies by this time tomorrow."

"But they can't shoot him."

"They can and they will. Thing's a monster. Ten feet tall. Eyes demon red. I hope they kill the thing 'fore sundown."

Billy tried to explain that it was a harmless chimp. That Sweet Potato was just a circus ape.

"These ol' boys wouldn't know an ape from a polecat hatched from a vulture's egg. I guarandarntee you that his hide's gonna be stretched out and his head's gonna be stuffed. Most ol' boys in these parts'd sell their soul for five hundred U.S. dollars."

Billy brooded, picking his teeth with a split toothpick. "What if I try to stop it?"

"You see these corned-up rowdies in here?"

Billy looked around and nodded.

"Mister, this ain't no quiltin' bee in here. They'll ride you out on a rail and whup the tar outta you."

"I reckon I'll take a pass on such fun."

"Mind if I ask you a question?" the bartender said.

Billy shrugged. "What?"

"Why you dressed like a goat?"

A plug-ugly old drunk stumbled up. "What the heck are you, the goat milk king?" The line of men down the bar guffawed. "Was your mama a critter?"

Billy paid him no mind. "You're drunk."

"And you're a goat."

The men gathered around, poking, gawking, pulling at the skins. For Billy, it was a bad scene about to get worse.

"You got any goat undies on under there?" a bat-eyed man with a silver dollar red birthmark on his face asked.

The fiddler on the small stage saw the brewing trouble. "Time for a break," he said, chomping down on his unlit cigar stub. He slipped his high button shoes back on and made for the exit.

The piano player agreed. He stopped plunking the cracked, stained ivories and finished his drink. With a practiced motion learned from too many saloon brawls he closed the lid, took a dip of snuff, emptied his tip cup and headed toward the back room for safety.

"I asked you a question," the man shouted, pushing Billy in the chest.

"Yeah, answer him," one of the bar women jeered, egging the crowd on.

Billy looked at his own face in the mirror. He tried to speak, but his voice was hoarse—nothing would come out. Seconds ticked away. He was in a pickle. There was no way he could fight all of them, and his circus buddies were miles away.

"Are you a goat or a chicken?" someone jeered.

"Keep away," Billy grumbled, pushing the man back. He tried to finish his drink, but the man shoved him against the bar.

"Come on out front and I'll knock the goat stuffin' out of you."

Billy paid him no mind. "Look, friend, I don't care a bean for havin' a go-round with you. Not a single ol' red-eyed bean. Not even an ol' string-bean, so leave me alone."

The drunk started making chicken noises. The crowd began whooping and hollering. "Fight! Fight!"

"Pick on someone your own size," Billy said, sliding off the stool.

The men looked down at the funny-looking dwarf. Then, from the back of the room, they pushed a small man in greasy jeans forward. "My name's Moose, and I'm your size," the little man said, his tongue sticking through the space where his front teeth should have been.

Billy turned a half circle, wondering how he'd get out of this one. The shouts and jeers bounced and ricocheted off the flimsy building.

"Fight! Fight!" The edgy men stomped their feet on the well-worn floorboards, fisted the bar, hooting and hollering for blood. They made so much clatter that the Star Tobacco sign came unhinged.

Billy looked toward the bartender for help. The crowd of drunk men was growing. The bartender knew that the intoxicated hilarity was one step away from fists flying. "Okay, boys, fun's over. No more cavortin' 'round. Go on back to your seats."

He leaned over to Billy and whispered, "Think you better get on outta here. Every man in here would take pleasure in poundin' on you."

Billy looked at the corned, whiskey-eyed men. They were breathing hard, muttering, crazy as loons, ready to snake their guns and have a go at him.

"I ain't gonna be your dead meat," Billy grumbled, knowing it was time to pull foot and head out. Without saying another word, he paid his tab and turned to face the crowd of men before him.

The small man went face-to-face with Billy. "Get 'em Moose," the crowd encouraged.

Billy had learned that the best fight is a quick fight. Knock someone senseless quick. Kick him into a cocked hat. Pummel him cold as a wagon tire, then hit the road.

Before Moose could get the first lick in, Billy grabbed him by the hair and wrestled him to the ground. They rough-and-tumbled over the floor, biting, kicking, gouging, spitting blood. Fur literally flew as Moose ripped up Billy's skin outfit. The crowd screamed, yelled, loving the two half-pints duking it out. Like two badgers, they cracked skulls and kneed each other until Billy got Moose in a deadly choke hold.

"You're killin' him," the bartender said, coming over the top.

Billy knew he had to prove his point now, or he'd have to fight every man in the room. He choked Moose harder and harder until he found himself lifted into the air by the sheriff, who happened to be passing by.

"Put me down!" Billy shouted.

"Stop throwin' a conniption fit." Sheriff Peterson looked around. "I want all you drunks and Missouri pukes to pay your bills and go home. This is a Christian town. No place for this sort of hoedown."

Moose stood up, dazed. "Let me at him," he whispered, punching the air. Someone flipped him an Arkansas toothpick. Moose looked at the long knife.

Sheriff Peterson shook his head. "Moose, 'fore you do somethin' and become a prison bad egg, I'm gonna ask you to drop the knife and go home and sleep it off." He looked around at the others. "That goes for all of you. No sense turnin' a headache into a jawbreaker."

Moose mean-eyed Billy, feeling the air come through where his britches had split plumb across his rear end.

The sheriff gave him the eye right back. "You want the Dutch beat outta you? That what you want?"

"No."

"Then settle this hash now, you hear?"

"Sorry," Moose grumbled, dropping the knife.

The men finished their drinks, grumbling that it wasn't fair, that the bigwigs were always ruining their fun.

"Pony up, boys," the bartender shouted, trying to collect the money owed him. They were still mumbling as they exited through the bat wing doors. Peterson carried Billy out the door and put him down in the middle of the street.

"Where you from?" the sheriff asked.

Billy started talking about apes and circus acts.

"Hold it, hold it," the sheriff interrupted. "Let's go to my office."

They drank coffee until he felt that Billy was sober enough to be believable. The sheriff listened politely to Billy's story about the lost ape, but he wasn't persuaded. "Look, Mr. Goat, I don't know what circus you rode in from, but this ain't no circus 'round here. We got folks half scared to death, lockin' their doors, boltin' their windows to protect their children. Believin' a monster's runnin' loose that's gonna chaw up the moon. And you're tellin' me that this Sweet, the Killer Ape from the Congo, is just some pet circus critter that loves to eat sweet potatoes?"

"That's right."

"I don't buy that. Not one bit. Dr. George said it tried to kill him. So did Henry Mead."

"But, Sheriff, all you have to do is find it for me, and I can take it back."

"Take it back in what? That goat wagon thingamajig you come ridin' into town on like some fairy tale come to life?"

"I can do it."

"Little man, you're not more than knee-high to a mosquito. Ape would make goat cheese outta the likes of you."

Billy was desperate and played his big card. "Look, there's a circus reward of five hundred greenbacks if I bring him back alive. I'll split that with you if you help me."

"Tippy may run a cheap drinking doggery, but he's put up his own good money."

"So am I."

"What you're offerin' comes up on the short end of the horn. Tippy's offered five hundred bucks for the creature dead and mounted on his wall. Probably throw in a year's worth of liquorin' to whoever does the killin'. You think these ol' boys 'round here would rather split the money with you or see them get the money and the brags of pointin' to the head of that thing hangin' over the bar?"

"But it's not right. They shouldn't be tryin' to kill Sweet."

"Folks got a right to protect themselves just like you folks had an obligation to keep that thing locked up. Now that you broke your obligation, I got an obligation to tell folks to use whatever force is necessary to protect their families."

"Even killin' a friendly animal?"

"Man alive, Mr. Goat. Folks 'round here have never seen an creature like this chimp you're describing. To them, it's the Mud Monster come to life."

"But it's just a chimp."

"To you it's a chimp or whatever you call it. To them it's like a swamp haunt comin' to life just once in their lifetime. Mark my words, boy, they'll be shootin' poppers and skyrockets when they drag it in dead."

42

Back Again

❖

The chimp sat in the tree, licking his wounds, looking down at the Springers' house. The smell of sweet potato pie was still all-consuming. Maybe these humans would be good to him. The little girl had treated him nice. Sniffing his coat, he hooted softly, glad to smell good again.

Life in the woods had been hard. Dogs had nipped at him. Humans shot at him, and a mean cougar had tried to kill him. Nothing like that had ever happened in his cage back at the circus.

Hearing the hunters' baying dogs, Sweet climbed a tall pine to see which direction the danger was coming from. Scared and upset, the chimp began hooting out his frustration to a world which had killed his mother, taken him from Africa, caged him, and now was hunting him.

Maurice stopped on his evening walk back from the barn when he heard the strange hooting sound followed by the roar of a cougar. Setting his bucket down, he broke open the breech of his shotgun to make sure it was loaded with two shells. He didn't care whether the ape liked sweet potatoes and would kiss you until Sunday; he wasn't taking any chances. He clicked the shotgun shut again.

"Eulla Mae, close that back door," he shouted. He saw a dark shape silhouetted high up in the tree in the fading light of day.

"What's wrong?" she called out, coming out onto the porch.

"You see that?" Maurice shouted, pointing to the tree line on the hill.

"What?"

"That. Up there. What is that thing?"

The cougar roared and the ape answered back. Eulla Mae felt her chest grow tight. Fear sparked in her eyes. "Get in the house, Maurice!"

"You go on in. I'm gonna find out what the heck's up there."

"You come in 'fore you get yourself killed."

"You think I'm scared? Why, girl, I've hunted boars and foxes and cottonmouth snakes and . . ." The cougar roared again, this time much closer.

Maurice looked around, talking softer. "And I've hunted snappin' turtles and deer and . . ."

The cougar's growl seemed just a few feet away. With barely a quicksilver second of hesitation, Maurice headed toward the house.

"Think there's more than an ape up there," he said as he took the porch steps two at a time.

Sweet climbed down from the tree and ran on all fours toward the creek in the ravine. The sharp rocks cut into his knuckles, but he didn't slow down. The cougar was following him.

Maurice and Eulla Mae stood on the porch, looking out into the dark. What had been a frightening chorus of animal cries was gone. Just the crickets talked among themselves, leaving Eulla Mae and Maurice to wonder if the ape would come back and what other danger was out there.

Billy rode up to the Springer farm to ask if he could use one of the pens for his goats and sleep in the barn.

"Don't think the men in town like me," he said, relating what had happened in the bar.

"You can sleep in the barn, no matter to me," Maurice said. "But you better keep them goats in there with you. We heard that hootin' sound again."

"You heard Sweet?"

"Not twenty minutes ago. And there's a cougar out there too."

Eulla Mae went to get blankets. Billy looked toward the dark woods. "Hope Sweet's okay. Maybe he'll come back 'round here in the morning."

The cougar roared, scaring the goats, and they began bleating. "Guess you're right 'bout keepin' them in the barn," Billy said.

"They'll keep you company," Maurice chuckled.

❖ ❖ ❖

An hour later, in the mist of the ravine, the cougar feasted. Hunkering down over the kill it had dragged along the rocks, the thick, earthy odor of dew-damp leaves mixed with the blood of the goat. The blood had already begun to crust. But it still wanted more. The big cat wanted the circus ape. Or a child.

43

Letter to "Heven"

❖

Darleda had counted to one hundred before she crept out of bed. Little Jim had been sent to sleep on the porch as punishment for wetting his bed and was out there in the dark all alone.

Little Jim wanted to cry. He was convinced that no one would want to adopt him. That his angel had gotten lost, or worse, maybe wasn't coming at all. All he wanted at that moment was to be held by Mrs. Wilson, but he knew he was all alone for the night. Maybe even for the rest of his life now that Darleda was most likely going to be taken on Adoption Day.

"Jim?" Darleda whispered out into the darkness. He didn't answer. She crawled out to the porch and found him staring at a spider crawling over his bad foot, like it wasn't a part of his body.

Brushing it away, Darleda comforted her friend, hoping he wouldn't get sick from the cold. *He's so frail. I've got to get him away from here before she kills him.* "You okay?" she asked.

"Just wonderin' where my angel is." They sat silently until he spoke again. "Darleda, if you get adopted, I'll never see you again."

"I won't leave if you don't leave with me." Darleda smiled.

"But no one's gonna adopt me."

"Sure they will. You've got more to give than any of us other kids." Little Jim looked down. "No one wants a crippled boy."

"If my daddy were here, he'd make you my brother."

"For real?"

"I know he would. I won't never, ever leave without you, Little Jim. That's my promise to you."

"You promise?"

"Cross my heart," she grinned. "You and me are kin now. Only heaven can keep us from being together on this earth."

"Wish your daddy would come back."

"He will. Don't worry."

"Think he'll make it back 'fore Adoption Day?"

"I said he'll be back. Now don't talk so loud or she'll hear us talkin'."

Little Jim looked at Darleda. She was the bravest person in the world in his eyes. He started to speak, then hesitated, like he was about to say something sinful. "Do you hate her?"

"Yeah, don't you?"

"I guess I should, but I remember that last time we was at church and the minister said hate only begets hate."

"Mrs. Robison's comin' unscrewed," Darleda argued.

Little Jim nodded, understanding her perfectly. "I do think her bolts are loose. She acts crazier than a bedbug dancin' on a match."

Darleda didn't want to worry the boy with her fears that worse was probably coming. The frail boy looked toward the star-filled sky. "You think God gets letters?" he asked.

"God gets whatever messages you send Him. Why?"

"Just wonderin'." He was worried that he'd done something wrong. Something to displease God. Then he grinned. "You like that Larry boy, don't ya?"

The blush on her cheeks couldn't be hidden by the dark. The moonlight accented the change in color. "Maybe."

"Like you like me?"

"You're more like a brother to me. Now, you get some sleep. I better get back inside before she does a bed check." Kissing his cheek, she left him her blanket and slipped back into the sleeping dorm.

Little Jim snuggled under the blanket, trying to ward off the dew-damp chill in the air. Watching the clouds cross over the moon, he felt courage, sending up a prayer to the angels he knew were somewhere up above with the stars. *My angel's up there. I know he's lookin' down on me. I don't care if it's a she angel. I just need an angel to rescue me.*

A night bird's call broke the spell. He took out his envelope. Carefully unfolding it, he read and reread the letter he'd composed:

Dear God:

Pleze hellp the kids livin here. They don't get no letters or have nough to eat. And they don't get to smile no more. Life waz good but now it is gettin kind of bad and there be worse to come. And I'm so tired of bein beat on. I feel like an old man in my boy body.

I want nothin cept for an angel to take me from here and find me a family. Can you send one for me? I don't got no mom or dad. I don't got nothin to speak of cept two ol shirts and one raggity pair of britches.

Ever cents the Rob-i sons took our rainbow away, I ain't felt good. It be like we don live heer no more. They r bad people who beat us for no reason. Kids ain't supposed to be treat-ted like this.

So when you read this, I want you to come into my room. I will wate for you. I will not slep. Just tell the angel to take me to a familiy. Someone who wants me. And would you bring Darleda's daddie back? She's my ownlee and bestest friend in the world.

Jim

Sealing it up, he wrote "God, Heven" on the envelope. Looking to see if Mrs. Robison was hiding in the bushes, he slipped off the porch and put the letter in the postbox up on the road. A shooting star crossed the heavens. The small, club-footed boy knew that God would send an angel to get his letter. The clouds that crossed the skies seemed to be carrying off his burdens. Little Jim was sure his angel would be coming soon.

Moral Distance

❖

The postman held the reins for the two-pony buckboard between his knees while he looked at the letter. It was addressed to "God, Heven." *Kids send the darndest things through the mail. Letters to Santa. Letters to Cupid. But this is the first one I've ever been asked to deliver up to heaven.*

At the Springers' house he stopped to chat with Eulla Mae and the funny-looking little man in goatskins. Billy was heading off into the woods to search for the escaped chimp. Terry and Sherry had offered to watch the goats and wagon.

The morning was half over when the postman got to the Younguns' house. He saw Rev. Youngun sweeping the porch. "Don't go wearin' yourself out," he said.

"Someone's got to keep up with the place," Rev. Youngun answered, leaning on the broom.

"That's what you got kids for."

"Mine do a disappearing act whenever they think work's coming up."

"I saw 'em over at the Springers. They're watchin' a goat wagon for a midget."

"I know. They talked about that silly wagon all night."

They chatted about the chimp and the Mud Monster stories going around. "My daughter says she gave the chimp a bath in the barn. Imagine that." Rev. Youngun tried to laugh but started coughing instead.

"Kids got great imaginations. And speakin' of which, I got a letter here that maybe you can deliver."

"Me?"

"Yeah, it's kinda in your field of work," the postman said.

"Who's it from?" Rev. Youngun asked, his curiosity piqued.

"It was over in the orphanage mailbox. Thought you might find it kinda cute." He handed the envelope to Rev. Youngun.

"I'll do what I can."

"Let me know what path you take. Might need to follow it myself one day," the postman chuckled, heading back up on the road on his route.

As Rev. Youngun read the letter in the kitchen, a wave of shame washed over him. As if he'd finally listened to a well-known secret. Something he should have known. He couldn't hide, couldn't close his eyes any longer. For all his sermons about moral darkness, about opening one's eyes to sin and pain, here it had been all along, not a mile away. Little orphan children were being abused and were crying out for help.

Did I close my ears? Did I not try to hear? Shame stabbed at his heart. The moral distance he had put between himself and the orphanage suddenly disappeared. The evidence was sitting right in his hand.

Orphans just want love. They just want to be part of a family. I should have cared more. Should have gone out there.

Larry's words hung in the air, a boy standing against the tide, telling his father there was something wrong just a mile away. He went up to find Larry, to apologize, but the boy was gone. Terry and Sherry were over at the Springers'. Rev. Youngun had never felt so alone.

Rising slowly, he turned toward the door. The room started spinning. The world blanked in and out. Rev. Youngun's head hit the door frame as he fainted.

Larry knew he shouldn't have gone, had promised he wouldn't go back, but he couldn't stop himself from guiding Lightnin' over the fields toward the orphanage. He was scared, and his hands trembled. He was crossing an invisible threshold in his life. There would be no turning back, no changing the face and facts of what he was doing.

Drawing deep breaths of the morning air to calm himself down, each step closer seemed to evaporate all his fears and doubts about the mission. The fall leaves grasped at the morning sunlight, soaking in the last growth light before nature turned them yellow-purple, sending them floating to the ground to rot. Larry rode on, believing in his mind that he was a knight going to save the fair lady. Like in the book, she was waiting for him with beckoning arms—only he wasn't too sure what that meant.

The warm sunshine gave him courage and strength. Almost made him cocky. He waved to several wagon loads of hunters who crossed the old ridge road, and he thought he saw a funny-looking man dressed in animal skins hiding in the brush.

"Must be that Billy Goat Man." Larry grinned, thinking about what his brother had told him about the neatest wagon in the world.

The whole world had turned topsy-turvy since yesterday's article in the newspaper about the Mud Monster. Larry wasn't sure what they were looking for, but he figured that between the lost chimp and the cougar tracks all the hunters trying for the reward would be lucky if they didn't go shooting themselves.

He guided the horse east to come in from the side, feeling like there was nothing in the world that could stop him now. But the feeling evaporated when he came upon Little Jim crying over the two slaughtered fawns.

"What happened?" Larry asked.

"The ape got them. The ape killed my deer," Little Jim cried.

Larry looked at the tracks. "I don't know about any ape. But those look like cougar tracks to me."

"But I saw the ape thing; he was here."

"When?"

"Two days 'fore last." Jim told him the story.

Larry traced the cat's print with his finger. "This is an Ozark mountain lion, a cougar. I'll swear to it."

"But I saw an ape. Right here. Lookin' at my fawns."

"All I know is that these are cougar tracks."

Jim shrugged. "I saw what I saw."

Larry looked toward the orphanage. "Where's Darleda?"

"She's cleanin'. Everybody's cleanin', doin' chores, gettin' ready for the Board meeting tomorrow." Jim scratched his head. "And Mr. Robison said we're gonna have fried chicken and taters tonight. Been a month of Sunday's since we had such a fine meal. Imagine that."

"Yeah, imagine that," Larry said, ashamed by how he had taken such simple things for granted in his life.

They buried what was left of the fawns, put up a makeshift cross, then sat on the rock together to talk.

"I didn't know this place was on the orphanage property," Larry said.

"It ain't," Little Jim said. "The barn belonged to that burnt-out house yonder."

"It's not on the orphanage property?"

"Nope. Told you that."

I didn't trespass. I didn't break my word to Pa. Larry decided that he'd ride home. He wouldn't be able to get to see Darleda today anyway. "You think you'll get adopted?" he asked.

"Told you before, no one would want me."

"I'd want you. Wish my dad would let you live with us."

"For real?"

"Sure. You're a good kid."

Jim brightened, happy at the thought that someone would actually want him, then took a breath. "I'd like that, but I promised Darleda that I'd be her brother. Think you could 'dopt her too?"

"Maybe. It'd be up to my pa."

"What's your pa like?"

"Well, he's kinda sick now, but he's a preacher and he's mostly fun."

Little Jim wiggled his club foot slowly. "Wish I knew what it'd be like to have a pa for my own. The kind of pa like Darleda talks 'bout."

"Wonder where her pa is?"

"That's somethin' I'm gonna have to ask my angel about."

Miles away, Darleda's father asked the conductor again how much time they'd have at the station. With the hours it had taken to clear the fallen tree off the tracks, they were pushing hard to get back on schedule.

"If you get right off and start ridin', you could get there by dark and head back in the morning. Can't wait the train beyond ten or they'll have my job," the conductor answered.

Ten. That gave him an extra hour. It would be just enough time to ride to Mansfield, find Darleda's grave, and gallop off.

45

Tired and Lonely

❖

Sweet looped through the woods on all fours, looking for more food. It was hard going over the strange territory. The last garbage dump had been picked clean by the rats and raccoons. Hunting dogs had nipped him. Almost caught him. The dogs that had ripped at his legs had wanted to kill. This wasn't a game. Sweet was panicked. Then he heard the mountain lion again.

Running through the knee-deep prairie grass which was thick with yellow flowers, Sweet stopped to pick at the tickseeds that covered his legs. He had never been this disoriented, never been in a place like this. Stumbling onto the thorn-studded pads of prickly pear plants, the chimp howled in pain. The thorns burned like hornet stings, digging deeper into his toes and hands with each stumbled step. He was upset. Tired and lonely. His stomach growled with hunger pains.

At the top of the ridge, Sweet heard more hunting dogs and hid within the branches of the red cedar trees that were loaded with pungent ice-blue berries. An instinct, some primal knowledge, said that the berries might cover over his scent.

A group of drunken hunters came running through the woods, yelling, laughing, warning every animal within a mile that they were coming with all the noise. One of the dogs sniffed at the tree where Sweet was, but then went after another animal and passed through the ravine, splashing along the creek. When their howls and baying had died off, the chimp pushed through the branches of scrubby oak and hickory, down to the glade. The cool ground carpet of leaves was easy on his feet, but he had to watch for the sharp, broken pieces of dolomite that were left from the creek that had once emptied into the marsh.

The dry creek bed made a convenient path, so the chimp followed it for a half mile, hidden by the forest that grew to the banks. Most of the trees were still oak and hickory, but here and there a sycamore and persimmon tree stuck through, their trunks covered with orange fungus and pale lichen.

Finding a patch of wild, graceful dogwoods, Sweet stopped to grab a lizard. But the lizard was too quick, scurrying away through the dry leaves between the rocks. There were wild turkeys, raccoons, and deer watching from a distance, but the creature paid them no heed. He wasn't fast enough to catch them.

Then he found food. A termite mound full of fat, squishy, white and brown crawling treats. Picking up a twig, he carefully stripped off the leaves and shoots, then pushed it deep into the mound. Probing around, letting the fat termites lock their jaws on the twig, Sweet slowly pulled it out. Like a line of hanging fish, the chimp licked each one off, crunching and swallowing, hooting with delight.

Moving on, he followed a fork on a deer trail, ending up in small creek. The cool water was refreshing. He drank, then tried to roll in the two-inch water to get the tickseeds off, but they were stuck like glue. He heard laughter from somewhere—human laughter—so he went up the rocky ridge on all fours, leaping from rock to rock. At the top, he heard the sounds but couldn't see over the trees. Jumping up to grab the thick tree branch, the chimp pulled himself to the top then looked around, trying to shake the clumps of mud that were hanging from his auburn coat.

Then he caught sight of Billy. The little man from the circus. Sweet hooted in happiness, trying to get the man's attention, but he was too far away. For the first time in a week the chimp had a direction to follow. He would try to catch up with the man from the circus.

Emergency

❖

Larry rode home at a gallop. He'd decided to sit down with his father and confess that he'd just about broken his word. To talk with him again about his fears.

"Pa, you upstairs?" he shouted as he came into the kitchen.

He found his father passed out in the doorway of the boy's bedroom. "Pa! Pa! What's wrong?"

His father blinked, groggy-eyed. "Lar . . . Larry. I must have fainted. Bumped my head."

Larry helped him to his feet. "You better get to bed."

"No. I'll be all right. Just get me to my chair downstairs." Rev. Youngun took two steps and almost fell again.

"Gotta get you to bed, Pa, then I'll call Doc George." His father leaned on him as they went down the hall.

Larry was scared.

Sherry and Terry rode up on Crab Apple the mule from visiting the Springers. Larry told them what had happened. Sherry ran crying to her room, screaming that her pa was dying.

"Hush up!" Larry ordered.

"I don't want to go to the orphanage," Sherry whimpered.

"You won't. Pa's just sick. But he'll get better if you shut your bawlin'."

Priming the pump, Larry let the water run in the sink until it was cold. Soaking the towel, he wrung it out and took it up and placed it carefully on his father's forehead.

"Thanks," Rev. Youngun said weakly.

Larry went back down to the kitchen and called Maurice, who rushed over. Then he called Dr. George, who came within the hour. After he'd felt Rev. Youngun's pulse, given him aspirin, and put another cold cloth on his head, Dr. George signaled for everyone to leave the room. They went down to the kitchen where the adults held counsel.

"He gonna be all right, Doc?" Maurice asked.

"Maurice, that man up there is exhausted. His body is worn out from the sickness," Dr. George said.

"Is he gonna be all right? Me and Eulla Mae, we're worried about him."

"I think he'll pull through. Some things just linger on," Dr. George said slowly.

"You *think?* What 'bout these kids? He can't be takin' care of them way he is," Maurice said.

"He needs all the help you can give him." Dr. George called the three children into the room. "You kids have to keep things under control. No running and jumping in the house. I don't want you to ask your father to do anything. Take responsibility and pull up your own socks for a while."

He turned to Larry. "You're the oldest. You have to be the man around the house now. Keep these other two from getting out of control and acting crazy."

"I will. I'll do my best," Larry said.

"And you two," Dr. George said, looking at Terry and Sherry. "No fighting or screaming. Your pa can't be bothered with things like that. He can't be coddling a couple of rascals. Peace and quiet is the only thing that will get him well."

"We'll take 'em over to our house," Maurice said to Dr. George.

"Is my pa gonna die?" Sherry asked.

"No. You don't need to worry about that," Dr. George said.

"Wanna hear 'bout what I saw in the barn?" Sherry asked suddenly, but everyone ignored her.

Terry gave her a head noogie when she came around the corner onto the porch. "Don't be tellin' any adults that you saw that chimp."

"Why not? It's true," Sherry said.

"Look, I've been tryin' to tell you that you were born nuts," Terry answered.

Sherry's mouth dropped open.

"That's right. Scrambled brains. Cracked. Crazy as a fruitcake. Loonier than a gooney bird."

"I'm not crazy," she blubbered.

"Yup you are. Doctor dropped you on the head when he took you from the stork's bag. Said your head squished up like a mush melon," Terry continued.

"You're lyin'."

"Swear it's true. They thought you was born in-sane."

"Liar, liar, pants on fire."

"Truth hurts but it's a fact. They had to scoop up your brains with a spat-tu-la and stuff 'em up your nose to get 'em back in. That's why Pa's always tellin' you not to blow your nose too hard. He don't want you blowin' your brains all over the room."

Sherry ran screaming into the kitchen, almost knocking Dr. George over. "Hush, girl. I told you not to carry on like that."

Maurice saw how upset she was and took her out onto the porch, smoothing her hair. "What's wrong, honey?"

"Terry said I was born in-sane."

Maurice saw Terry peeking around the corner. "Boy, don't you be tellin' your sister such things. It'll scare her half to death."

"Did not. Said she was born to raise cane," Terry explained.

"Hope lightnin' don't strike you dead, Red. One day you're gonna go the whole hog and regret it."

"Sorry, Mr. Springer."

"Can't you ever jus' once say somethin' nice to your sister?" Maurice asked.

Terry thought for a minute. "I made up a poem for her."

Sherry closed her eyes. "No. Don't want to hear it."

"Is it nice?" Maurice asked.

"It's a poem, ain't it?" Terry said, shrugging his shoulders like a camel walking.

"Say it then," Maurice sighed.

"Okeydokey, here it is:

"Roses are red,
Violets are blue,
Sherry's got the kind of face

That you wipe off your shoe."

Sherry started crying again. Maurice picked her up and looked at her brother.

"You're just a sugar sneakin' meanie," she whimpered.

"Geesh, ain't every day that someone gets a poem made up 'bout 'em," Terry complained.

Maurice brought Terry and Sherry into the kitchen.

"You two kids remember," the doctor said, "don't make a lot of noise. That man upstairs is sick."

"We'll be good, Dr. George, don't worry," Terry said.

After the doctor left, Maurice went up and sat by the bed. Rev. Youngun was pale, and his breathing was labored.

"Thanks," he whispered.

"No need thankin' me. You just get yourself better," Maurice said.

"Never fainted before."

"First time for everything. Now, you get some sleep. I'm gonna go get Eulla Mae and bring some supper back for you and the kids."

Terry and Sherry rode with Maurice back to the Springer farm. Terry leaned over and whispered to Sherry, "You're adopted."

"I am not."

"What's he sayin' to you?" Maurice asked. Sherry told him. "Did you tell your sister that?"

"Naw, she heard it all wrong. I said the wagon's lopsided."

"Boy, you're faster with the mouth than an auctioneer drinkin' coffee."

"Guess that's a com-plee-ment," Terry grinned.

"You can't trick ol' Maurice any sooner than you can catch a weasel asleep."

47

Strong Medicine

❖

Terry wanted to stay at the Springers' and pretend to drive the goat wagon, but Maurice thought it best not to leave him alone. "That wildcat out there might eat you up if he caught you."

Eulla Mae came back with them in the wagon, carrying a covered dish, fresh-made snake root and wahoo tea, and a bottle of Compton's Sassafras Patent Medicine. She fretted all the way over about Rev. Youngun's health, warning the kids not to act crazy. When they got to the Younguns' house, Eulla Mae went directly up to the patient.

The sassafras medicine tasted terrible. "That's awful," Rev. Youngun coughed, reaching for the glass of water.

Eulla Mae read the label. "Says here that it cures consumption, bronchitis, whooping cough, yellow fever, loose bowels, and cholera. Here, take another spoonful."

"No more. Please," he said, covering his mouth.

Sherry sat downstairs with Maurice and told him about bathing the ape. "You got a good imagination, girl, I'll give you that." Maurice smiled, tossing her into the air.

"But I saw it. I saw it."

Eulla Mae had heard the story and grinned. She picked Sherry up from Maurice's lap. "I'm sure you did. Now run on back to your room and play. We want to get dinner ready."

No matter how hard they tried, they couldn't keep Rev. Youngun from coming down.

"You just sit then," Eulla Mae ordered.

"I feel better now," Rev. Youngun said weakly.

"You lift a finger, and Maurice and I'll just have to lift you back into bed like a baby."

"Yes, ma'am." He smiled.

She heated water and did the pile of dishes on the sideboard. Then she straightened up the icebox and started a pot of coffee. Each time Rev. Youngun tried to lend a hand, Eulla Mae shooed him away. He started to stand, but she put her hand on his shoulder. "You just sit there."

"But I'm not helpless," he said weakly. A bead of sweat hung above his lip.

"You're still sick. Look weak as a baby. If you don't get your strength back, you might never get better."

"You're the doctor," he smiled, wondering how he was so lucky to be blessed with such neighbors.

They talked about neighbors, the weather and crops. Maurice again retold the story about Terry saving Sherry in town. "What that boy won't do for a gumdrop," he concluded.

"He's got a sweet tooth." Rev. Youngun grinned, then turned serious. "If anything were to happen to me, I want . . ."

Eulla Mae interrupted him. "Don't be talkin' about such things. You be bringin' on bad luck 'fore you know it."

"I just wanted to ask you a favor."

"What?" Maurice asked, sitting down.

"Just, that if something were to happen to me, I'd like to ask you both if you would take in my children."

They sat stunned.

"You mean raise 'em?" Maurice asked.

"Raise them as your own."

Eulla Mae started crying. "You know we would. You know we love them kids as if they were our own."

"I know you do. That's why I wanted to ask you before I put it in my will," Rev. Youngun said.

Maurice started chuckling. "Imagine me and that redhead sneakin' 'round the house, seein' who'd get first licks on Eulla Mae's pies." It was one of those moments of pure pleasure before reality set in.

"But what 'bout the law?" Maurice asked. It put a damper on the moment.

"That won't be a problem. I'm talking to the lawyer," Rev. Youngun answered confidently. But even he was unsure of what would happen.

"Law's a funny thing, Reverend," Maurice said quietly. "A law can mean one thing for white folk and another for blacks."

"But they're just children." Eulla Mae sniffed. "They'd need a home."

"Let's see what the lawyer says," Rev. Youngun began. "I think things can be worked out legally. Hopefully, pray to God, I'll get better. But I've never been sick this long. It makes you think. Makes you worry about the future."

"We're here whenever you need us. You know that," Eulla Mae said, hugging the sickly man.

"That's all a man can ask."

He told them about what Larry had said was going on at the orphanage and about the strange feeling he'd gotten from Mr. Robison when he came by the house. Then he showed them the letter from Little Jim and worried aloud that he was too sick to go over there himself.

"You think Larry saw what he says?" Maurice asked.

Eulla Mae nodded. "She's a mean one, she is. I saw the way her eyes flared in town. Didn't even say one thank you to Larry for tryin' to stop their wagon."

"Tomorrow I'll call the Board members and the sheriff. Someone's got to do something."

"Too bad you didn't talk to Dr. George 'bout it when he was here. He's on the Board, ain't he?"

"Yes. I should have. Guess I'm not thinking clearly," he said, closing his eyes. Eulla Mae looked at Maurice with concern.

"I heard that Robison woman whups on them kids pretty good," Maurice nodded, looking away, almost embarrassed by the revelation.

"Who told you that?" Rev. Youngun asked.

"Henry Mead. He's kinda a handy man 'round the orphanage. Says no worries 'bout spoilin' them kids since she don't spare the rod for nothin'." Maurice poured himself coffee from the pot.

"How bad did he say it was?" Rev. Youngun asked.

"Said even on the worse days when his pa used to whup up on him, he was never whipped 'round like that."

The words hung in the air. All were embarrassed for having closed their eyes to what should have been obvious.

"I think there's more than discipline going on out there," Rev. Youngun said quietly. It was a revealing moment of truth.

Maurice nodded. "We all heard the whispers. Why, your Larry saw things. Told us all. But we didn't really listen, did we?" He looked at his shoes. "No one listens much to kids."

"I'm guilty of that. I didn't listen to Larry," Rev. Youngun affirmed.

Maurice cleared his throat. "If this be truth-tellin' time, guess this child will admit that every town's got three things. A church, an American flag, and a well-known secret 'bout a man half-beatin' his kids to death that no one does nothin' about."

The Springers took Terry and Sherry back with them to their farm. Larry was left to watch over his father.

48

Sweet Sight

❖

Sweet followed Billy from a distance, knowing it was the same human who used to feed him when he lived in the cage. Scratching himself, he hooted softly, but the little man didn't turn around. Tossing a rock down the ravine, he tried to get the man's attention. The rock slid unheard down the smooth face worn down by the river that once flowed through.

Billy turned for a moment, looked around, then moved back into the forest, which swallowed him.

Sweet stopped abruptly, sniffing the air. Hair bristling, he spun around, wondering where the danger was. Across the small ravine he saw the cougar again.

The chimp hooted, trying to threaten away the cat, showing he was the boss in a display of aggression. The cougar roared back, whipping its long tail back and forth, uncurling it, snapping it back like a bullwhip. The cat had been following at a distance all day and was determined to catch the thing that walked upright. The cat could smell it, almost taste it, but the cat couldn't jump across the wide expanse that separated them. Howling again, muscles rippling along its satiny, yellow skin, it batted the air with its front paw, showing off the thick scars on its head from fierce fights it had won.

Instinct told the chimp that this cat would hurt him, maybe kill him. So he kept moving, trying to find familiar ground but keeping his distance from the cat who was desperate to jump over the ravine. Then he turned and saw the cougar, legs spread like eagle's wings, its thick tail thrashing the air. Hooting in panic, Sweet jumped up and down, desperate to scare the cat off.

The cat wasn't scared. The chimp's jumping and hooting made it want the kill even more. Muscles tensed, the cat's paws clawed at the edge of the steep incline, it spun around, moved back ten feet, then bounded back and leaped into the air.

Sweet panicked, reaching for the limbs above but they were out of reach. The cat hit the ledge, then slipped down, digging its claws into the rock. The chimp beat at the cougar's paws until it let go, tumbling to the bottom.

Knowing he should run, curiosity drove Sweet to peek over the edge, to make sure the creature had really fallen. Hooting out one last challenge, the chimp ran off, jumping until he grabbed on to a tree branch, then moved through the woods, trying to find the way back. Trying to catch up with the little man who smelled like goats. But Sweet was lost, and he didn't know how to get back to the only home he had ever known.

Inspection

❖

After the Springers left with Terry and Sherry to take them back to their house, Rev. Youngun called Dr. George and told him about Little Jim's letter. Dr. George said he had to see a patient who lived out by the orphanage. "You want me to stop over there and check on those kids?"

"If you can. I'd sleep better knowing they're okay."

"I think you're making a big worry out of nothing," Dr. George said.

"I don't think so."

"I'll go on over there, but you promise me that you'll get in bed and stay there. Sheriff Peterson's gonna be riding with me, so we'll both look around."

Out of courtesy Dr. George called ahead and told Mr. Robison his plans.

"Come on out anytime. We're always glad to have you here." Robison was upbeat, feeling like he was about to change his life, to see sunshine instead of dark clouds.

By coincidence that night the orphans were served the best meal they'd had since Mrs. Wilson left. Tasty fried chicken, mashed potatoes, fried apples with all the fixin's, brown sugar on the green apples, and all the sweet milk they could drink. Mr. Robison had done it all and served up Dr. George and the sheriff Sunday-sized helpings.

"More, please," Little Jim said, taking another piece of chicken.

"Eat up, children," said Mr. Robison, feeling good, having taken the first step to ease his conscience.

The kids took turns sitting on the sheriff's lap, looking at his badge, touching his holster. Each of the children was introduced to him, while Dr. George was given a tour of the property.

Darleda opened the cover of Larry's dime novel and wrote him a message, thanking him and telling him to come back and see her. She figured that either the doctor or the sheriff knew him, so she introduced herself to the sheriff, asking him if he knew the Younguns.

"Sure. Rev. Youngun. He's the Methodist minister."

"Would you give his son Larry this?" she asked, handing him the dime novel. "Tell him thanks."

"Why don't you tell him that yourself?"

"Wish I could. But we don't get to come to town anymore."

"I'll give it to him. And I'll pass on your message." He didn't ask how the two of them had gotten together but suspected they were sweet on each other.

Mr. Robison took Dr. George around the grounds, showing him the dorm rooms, the barn, and the storage sheds. He did want to change his ways, to be nicer to the children, but there was also self-interest at the heart of it. If Dr. George saw that the kids were unhappy and told the other Board members, maybe he and Sarah would be prevented from straightening out their lives. His wife needed help, in his mind there was no question. But he'd never be able to help her if she was taken away to an institution.

While the children played games and sang, Sheriff Peterson stood with Mr. Robison and Dr. George by the corner fireplace, sipping coffee. "These are good kids," he said.

"I think so," Mr. Robison answered.

Dr. George looked at a girl with a runny nose. "Guess we need to schedule a checkup for the kids."

"Been about a year," John Robison said slowly.

"Kids should be checked on twice a year at least."

"We've just been so busy, but I won't let it slip again." Two little girls played jacks in front of the crackling logs. Laughter was in the air for the first time in a year. *This is what we should have been doin' all along,* John told himself.

"Kids seem real happy." Dr. George smiled, looking around. "You say that Mrs. Robison's not feeling well?"

"Headaches. Guess it comes with her age."

"Tell her to come to my office. I've got some pain powders which work real well," Dr. George said.

Then he used the orphanage phone to call Rev. Youngun and assured him that everything was fine.

"The kids are happy?" Rev. Youngun asked.

"Seem happy to me. Ate a good dinner. Played games with the sheriff. Mr. Robison seems like a good man."

"What about Mrs. Robison?"

"She's got a headache. But if she's like him, guess we don't have anything to worry about. Now you just take care of yourself and get some rest."

After the doctor and the sheriff had left, Robison felt that he could make it through the Board meeting if Sarah would stay in bed. That he had covered over any worries that the doctor might have arrived with.

Darleda came over to him. "The children are happy you're doin' this."

"I'm glad."

"They all look full as ticks."

"Mr. Robison," Little Jim called out, "let's eat like this every night."

"Be thankful for what the Lord provides," Mr. Robison said.

Darleda stood watching the children play pass-the-shoe. Smiles. Laughter. It was as the orphanage used to be.

"My turn!" squealed a girl in pigtails. She put the napkin in her shoe. "Get ready." The circle of kids tightened up in anticipation.

"Onesee, twosee, zim-zim-zam," the girl shouted as the circle group banged their shoes together.

"Bobtail, vinegar, pickle in the pan.
Pick it, choose it, wish for luck,
Now get ready and pass the buck!"

At the word *buck* they madly passed and grabbed shoes around and around while the girl continued.

"Army, navy where's the buck?
If you got it you're out of luck!"

They fell together in squeals, each one hoping they hadn't ended up with the napkin in the shoe.

"Where's Mrs. Robison?" Darleda asked Mr. Robison, worried that the woman would storm in and break up their fun.

"She's sleeping. She needs her rest." He looked at the girl through new eyes. "Guess you don't like her much, do ya?"

"She doesn't like me, that's for sure."

"Well, maybe you'll get a new family on Adoption Day."

"Nope, my daddy's comin' back." Her faith in her father was unshakable. "Mr. Robison, can we celebrate Jim's birthday later?" Darleda asked.

"If you don't make too much noise."

"We won't." She paused, searching for the right words. "Mr. Robison?"

"Yes?"

"I don't want to be put up for adoption. My father could still come back."

"He could, but it's been a year. Law says we're supposed to find you a good family."

"Where do you think my father is?"

"This is a big country. No tellin' where he might be."

Darleda went back to her dorm, trying to accept the fact that her father wasn't coming back. That he wouldn't make it back before the one-year deadline when she could legally be put up for adoption.

Less than ten miles away, Robert Jackson kept the horse to a fixed gallop, stopping only for water. There wasn't much time. The train wouldn't wait beyond ten the next day. Mansfield was still a couple of hours away. He figured that he could rent a room at the hotel and be at Darleda's grave by dawn. Say his piece, take a picture with his mind, and then ride on back and take the train west toward Denver.

He checked the rifle straps under his bedroll. This was a lonely road. No telling what he might run into.

Unhappy Birthday

❖

Darleda walked into the boys' sleeping dorm for Little Jim's birthday party. It was nothing special, just homemade gifts and bits of fruit they'd saved from their meal. Just small gifts from their hearts, which was all that counted.

But as children will, they made noise. At first it was quiet whispers and giggles, then it got louder and louder with singing and games.

When Mrs. Robison first entered the room, she smiled, going around the room, inspecting the pitiful little gifts. Then, without warning, she squeezed Little Jim's arm, telling him that she'd be back, then she disappeared from the room. The boy had known that something bad was going to happen, but he didn't know when. All he could do was creep into bed and lie there hoping that he didn't wet his sheets.

"What's she gonna do, Darleda?" he whispered.

"I don't know. Maybe nothin'."

A minute passed. Then another. The waiting was a killer, sapping their strength.

Darleda left the dorm and found Mr. Robison out by the barn. "She came in."

"What?"

"Mrs. Robison came into our party. Found us singing to Little Jim."

"And what did she say?"

"She squeezed Little Jim, hard, then said she'd be back."

"I'll go talk to her."

When Darleda got back to the boys' room, she saw the shape by the sleeping dorm door. Saw a dark hat cross the light as the old grandfather clock in the main house chimed out nine bells. Pulling herself up to the window ledge, she hissed out, "Psst, Jim, she's back."

"She's gonna whup me," Little Jim whimpered.

"Just don't say anything to upset her. She's crazier than a cuckoo clock."

Little Jim held his breath, pretending to be asleep with his clothes on, clutching the sheets. Too afraid to open his eyes, his heartbeat matched the clump of her thick-soled black shoes as she came down the center of the dorm. The kerosene lamp hanging from the center ceiling clinked with each step.

Boom, boom, boom.

She looked at the presents they'd made, her brain screaming for relief. Her husband had told her to leave the children alone, but she was determined to find out what they were doing.

Boom, boom, boom.

"Happy birthday to you," she sang softly, the muscles in her face drawn sharp. Her mind was caught up in silent, lunatic rhythms.

Jim started to moan.

"Happy birthday to you."

She stopped at his bed. Little Jim's flesh began to crawl. Mrs. Robison screamed loudly, demanding that he respond, but he was so scared that all he could do was shake and stutter. "Don . . . don't hur . . . hur . . . hurt me."

"Speak normal," she commanded. The entire dorm seemed to shudder with the laughter of the terrible woman. She grabbed Little Jim's bad foot and squeezed.

For the first time in his life, Jim fought back, the rage of being life's runt overpowering his common sense born of intimidation. "Get off!" he shouted, kicking her away.

Darleda ran into the room. "Leave him alone!" she begged. "He's not feelin' well."

"And soon he'll feel worse," the woman sneered. "I'm gonna teach him not to talk during chores."

Putting his hands together, Little Jim prayed silently. *Please God. I don't want to be hurt no more. Take me to heaven.*

"Stop praying!" Mrs. Robison raised her hand to slap him.

"No, don't!" Darleda screamed, trying to hold Mrs. Robison's clammy hand back.

"Don't touch me," the woman hissed, pushing Darleda away, unable to stop the monster from crawling out from under her skin. She looked around, her eyes unsure, unfocused, deranged. Darleda watched in revulsion, fighting back the thoughts in her mind of hitting the woman. Of avenging all the wrongs. For chopping off her hair. She knew such thoughts were bad, probably sinful, but she felt like she was trapped in a nest of black widow spiders and the only way to save herself was to fight back. "Do something," Darleda shouted to the bigger boys. But they stood mute, afraid that Mrs. Robison would turn her wrath on them.

Someone's got to do something, Darleda thought, pleading with her eyes for the boys to stand up for Little Jim who lay there cowering. She watched the woman cock her fist, ready to hit the frail boy, her face so flushed that the sweat beads looked like blood.

"Leave him alone," Darleda said, standing between them.

"Move out of my way." The pain was spreading in all directions like river ice cracking. Sarah Robison's demon was about to crawl out. She pushed Darleda away and went after Jim who was trying to crawl under the bed.

Darleda couldn't stand it. Calling up courage and the instinct to survive, to do what was right, Darleda grabbed the woman's arm, shaking it loose from Jim's leg. From somewhere in the hills a coyote called out, then another, then another, like they sensed the fight going on inside the orphanage. A gust of violent wind shook the windows. The children crept out of their beds to watch. Darleda had crossed a boundary from which she could never return.

They grappled in slow motion. Darleda jumped at Mrs. Robison's face but was kneed down. She felt the breath whoosh from her lungs but still she struggled, desperate for freedom. To fight back against this evil woman. A pillow got between them, and stuffing flew everywhere. Then, with a stunning backhand, Mrs. Robison knocked the girl down, laughing as Darleda banged her head against the wall, her breath whooshing out again. For a moment the girl was too dizzy to speak, her eyes watering in pain. She was woozy, sick to her stomach. Her hands were trembling, and her left leg jerked involuntarily.

"Leave her alone," Little Jim pleaded.

Mrs. Robison walked slowly before the assembled children. Little Jim had not gotten up. His heart thumped in fear.

"When we have the Board meeting, I want each of you to be on your best behavior, do you understand?"

The children nodded.

"I don't want any of you tellin' stories, trying to make me look bad. Is that clear?" She spun around toward Darleda. "That includes you." They locked eyes, each acknowledging her true feelings.

"Those that get adopted out, will leave with their new families on Adoption Day. Those that don't will find that if you're good, we'll have fried chicken every week, and I'll let you have Saturday afternoons for games." The children's faces brightened. "It'll be a new beginning."

It was all lies.

"Does that mean you won't hit us anymore?" Darleda asked.

Mrs. Robison felt the first stab in her head.

Boom, boom, boom.

It was coming.

Boom, boom, boom.

She wanted to blink, wanted to lie down. It took all her strength to focus on the girl.

Her cruel laughter seemed to lock the doors and windows around them. She spun around, out of control, babbling, talking to herself. The children watched, frozen with fear. "No one cares about orphans. No one. When will you understand that?" she shouted, the veins standing thick against her neck.

She put her finger against Darleda's nose. "The present I have for you is what you've been wanting. You know what it is?"

Darleda shook her head.

"Since your father abandoned you, I've made arrangements for you to be adopted out."

"By who?" Little Jim whispered, worried that he was going to lose his only friend in the world.

"By who?" Darleda echoed.

"By me!" Mrs. Robison screamed, howling with laughter. "I'm gonna adopt you and raise you myself."

"No. You can't!"

"Yes! You'll be my daughter," the woman hissed. Her anger was a terrible thing to behold.

"You can't keep me."

"I can and I will." Mrs. Robison walked over to Darleda, ready to strike her again, but her husband came into the dorm and grabbed her arm.

"Enough! Stop, Sarah! Stop!" he shouted.

Mrs. Robison's eyes flared at him, like she was about to claw his eyes out. Then a dead calm came over her. "All right. It's over."

Darleda stifled a sob. Her head throbbed, her breath came in rumbling bursts. A goose-egg knot had formed on the back of her head.

Little Jim crawled over to Mr. Robison. "Don't let her hurt me no more. Please."

The man looked at the fear on the children's faces. He saw what he'd ignored all these years and was heartsick to his soul. "She won't hurt you, boy." He turned to Sarah. "Leave us alone. I want to say my piece to the children."

No one spoke as she walked from the room.

"What's wrong with her?" Little Jim asked, afraid that the man might hit him but wanting answers to what was beyond his comprehension.

"She's got problems. I can't explain them, but God willin', I'll find someone who can help her."

Darleda mustered up her courage again. "She's crazy. You know that, don't you?"

John Robison was silent. Not wanting to admit it to the children. A moth bounced around the light. "She's not been right since she lost our daughter."

"What daughter?"

"Darley. Our twelve-year-old daughter who died from diphtheria. She's grieved for a long time. You remind her of Darley," he said to Darleda.

"That's no excuse."

The trapped moth dropped down, searching for a way out.

"I said, she's not been right. Has bad headaches. Now let's take a look at your cuts."

She's a loony. Ought to be locked up, Darleda thought in a flash of adult understanding, wishing her father was back in her life when she had that everyday safe feeling. She sat quietly while the man lightly twisted and poked around the purple lump at the hairline above her right eye.

"I'll be all right. Just go fix Little Jim."

"Keep a cold cloth on it." He gave her a serious look. "You got grit, child."

There was a medicine box and rags in a corner basket. He took out the bottle of iodine and soaked the rags in the wash pitcher. "This is gonna hurt," he said to Little Jim. Darleda was waiting, watching. It was the first sign of hope in the Robisons she had seen.

Mr. Robison talked quietly about life, about how some people have troubled minds. How losing the child had messed up his wife. How Darleda looked very much like his daughter. "All people are precious to the Lord. With time, she'll get better."

Darleda listened politely, but she knew that the ground was falling out from under them all. That you couldn't curtain off your memory or the feeling that something bad was going to happen.

51

Overdue Call

❖

John Robison put the children back to bed, listened to them say the Lord's Prayer, then called for lights out and trudged back to the main house. It was the decision point he'd never wanted to face. Sarah's illness had to be confronted—now. She had snapped and was dangerous. They had to talk, but she was asleep, curled up, whispering gibberish. He stared at the ceiling, knowing that he'd let it get out of control. *Should have told someone. Should have gotten her help.*

He went to the kitchen, picked up the telephone, and asked the operator to connect him with Rev. Youngun. He waited, listening to the crackling on the line and the rifle reports ricocheting between the ravines outside the window. The hills were alive with hunters.

"Sorry to call you so late, Rev. Youngun," he began.

"That's all right. Dr. George called and said the children all seemed very happy. When I get to feeling better I'd like to come visit myself." All he could assume was that the letter had been just a lonely child's thoughts.

Robison answered with his silence.

"Is there something wrong, John?"

Robison hesitated. "There are things we need to talk about. Things you need to know. My wife needs help, needs help bad. She's never gotten over losing our daughter."

All Rev. Youngun's worries came back as Robison spoke. It was the first step out of the swamp of darkness. Like a pent-up river of emotion, Robison broke through and told everything. From the beginning. About Darley, the asylum, about being fired from other orphanages, the lies, the bad spells, and the children Sarah had hurt. "I've been hidin' it so long that it just all started seeming natural," he concluded.

"God can bring anyone back from the abyss who gives his or her life over to Him," Rev. Youngun whispered. "He's the best hope for her."

"We've tried faith healers, doctors who probed her. None of it worked," John replied.

"Dr. George might know of cures you haven't heard of."

"Maybe there's no cure for what ails her. You can't take back the past and make a person whole."

"No, you can't."

Tears came to John's eyes. "I've let Sarah get outta hand. Shoulda stopped her. She beat on them somethin' fierce tonight." He told Rev. Youngun everything that had happened.

"I think we should call Dr. George. Have him come get her."

"She's scared of being locked away again. This time they probably won't let her out."

"She could have killed Darleda." Silence hung after his words. "We have to think of the children first, John, that's important. Then we'll see about what we can do for Sarah."

Larry listened to his father's end of the conversation from the dark hallway, his heart beating fast. He knew that something bad was happening at the orphanage. Fear pulled at him. There would be no sleep. *I've got to go over there. I've got to help Darleda*, he thought, taking off his nightshirt and tugging on his boots.

Slipping out of the bedroom window, he crawled along the porch. Hanging off the edge, he dropped to the ground, ran to the barn and quickly saddled Lightnin'. Dangit the dog wanted to tag along, but Larry shooed him away. The horse was skittish, didn't want to go, but Larry pulled him by the reins until they were down past the mailbox. The stars told him that night still had a long way to go.

He rode off into the dark. Somewhere in the hills a coyote talked to the moon. Larry didn't hear the cougar answer back. But his horse did. Lightnin's head and ears twitched and twisted as he listened to the dark.

52

Ride Through the Hills

❖

Terry slipped out to the barn to see if Billy was asleep yet. Since everyone was watching him like hawks during the day, he figured that if he could get the goat wagon out of the barn, he could take it for a little spin without anyone being the wiser.

Billy was sawing thick logs, snoring, snorting, sounding like hornets in a barrel. Terry took his time, whispering to the goats as he hitched up the forty-goat team, "Gonna be fun. Gonna race the moon."

Easing open the barn door, he looked to see if the Springers were awake. It would have been fun havin' someone, even Sherry, to ride with him, but he figured she'd rat so he had to go alone.

It was candle-lighting time. The dark would cover him. Terry got into the teeny wagon and raised up the whip. "Okay you can-eaters, get ready to move."

Twenty goats suddenly turned their heads and looked at him. Terry felt goose flesh forming for no reason. The goats seemed spooked about something. The other twenty goats started bleating. "Quiet, hush, 'fore you wake up the man who skinned your kin."

He felt a tap on the shoulder. He turned, expecting to see Sherry, but it was the ape.

"You're the ape," he whispered, too scared to move.

Sweet hooted, feeling Terry's auburn hair.

"I think I better go off to sleep now."

Sweet stuck a finger into Terry's ribs, tickling him.

"Hey, cut that out," he giggled.

When the ape crawled up into the wagon, the goats started bleating loudly enough to wake the dead. Maurice threw open the window. "What in tarnation's goin' on?"

Billy stumbled from the barn and saw the chimp. "Sweet! You're back!"

Then they heard the cougar roar from the hills. Sweet started jumping up and down in the wagon, hooting loudly. The goats got more scared. Maurice shouted louder. Billy shouted even louder. Terry tried to climb out of the wagon but fell backward as the forty-goat team took off toward the hills.

Terry grabbed the side of the wagon and knew he was in trouble. Maurice was running down the road after them. Billy was screaming that the kid had stolen his wagon. Sherry and Eulla Mae stood on the porch, and the chimp was hooting like a steam whistle.

"Stop! Let me off!" Terry yelled.

All he could do was hold on for dear life. The goats had a mind of their own. Where they were going was anybody's guess. They flew along the dark road heading for Mansfield. Every time Terry shouted for the goats to stop, the chimp would hoot and double hoot, scaring them to run even faster.

Then the chimp kissed Terry, a big fat wet one.

"Stop that!" Terry exclaimed.

Sweet wrapped his arms around the boy.

"Hey, I ain't your sweetie."

Terry wished he'd never gotten into the wagon. That he had stayed in bed like Maurice told him to. He looked around. The moon was out. The woods were dark. He was in a wagon with a kissin' chimp. There was only one word he could say: "Help!"

53

Sarah in the Dark

❖

Sarah sat in the dark, her disturbed mind racing down a dark and twisted road in hell. Shadows glided through the room. Shapes formed. Cobwebs closed around her. The room spun then turned over.

Her hair was a rat's nest. Spittle clung to her lower lip. She needed to rest, to sleep, to not think about the bad things. But the thoughts came back with the pounding in her head.

He wants to lock me back in the asylum. I'm not going to let them stick pins into me. Wrap me in wet sheets. Tie me to the bed.

"Sarah, where are you?" John called out. His heart hurt with the truth.

She sat silent, shivering, chewing on her lip, looking for a place to hide. In her mind John was an enemy who wanted to lock her away.

"Sarah, are you all right?" he called again, wishing he could erase her terrible past.

"Go away."

"Let me in."

"No. Go away, I said."

John stood outside the door. Shaking his head, he knew it was over. She needed to be under a doctor's care. Maybe even be put in a rest home or asylum until she got better. "Get some sleep. Please. We'll go see the doctor in the morning." There was nothing he could do except silently mourn for her.

She listened for the floorboards to creak to let her know that he had walked away from the door. Three minutes clicked by before she heard the wood groan as he trudged off to their bed. Her eyes glowed with conviction. In her sewing box were the long, sharp scissors. Walking slowly, Sarah went to the table and opened her sewing kit. The scissors felt cold. Lifting them up, she feathered the blades back and forth. The crack of moonlight reflected off them. Walking toward the door, she raised the scissor high.

Robert Jackson rode hard down the last leg to Mansfield. He was tired and hungry. He was a sullenly handsome man with a two-day beard that didn't feel good to his touch. *Need a two-bit shave and a haircut. Must look a bad sight.*

The can of sardines he'd eaten in the saddle hadn't done much for his hunger without bread and cheese. The last road ranch he'd passed didn't have anything to trade except rancid salt pork. The hucksters selling wares from the back of wagons weren't much better. They had wanted to cheat him.

Money-suckin' grubs, he thought. *Wanted a dollar for a piece of salt hog and a soggy corn dodger. Probably steal pennies off a dead man's eyes.*

The few dollars in his pocket were precious. Alone in the world, Jackson needed every cent to get his new life going. His clothes hung loose, would have looked like skin and bones if it hadn't been for the hard-packed muscles that still held his frame tight. His stomach growled for food, but it would have to wait.

The early night air was cold. His horse was lathered and breathing heavily. They'd stopped only once to splash water. Jackson was glad he'd picked the roan and not the mare with worn molars and the cloudy left eye. The ride had taken longer than he'd planned on, and he was now worried that he wouldn't make it back to the train by ten. He booted the horse to gallop faster, heading northeast past the tired roads leading to Ozark hill families going nowhere fast. The abandoned farms. Past the crumbling shacks, half hidden by willow trees and waist-high brown weeds.

Can't miss the train. Gotta get to Denver.

There was next to no one on the streets of Mansfield. *Guess they're all quiltin' or singin' hymns.* It looked like a Bible-thumping kind of town. His horse snorted and pulled as he passed by the livery, but there wasn't time to let him have a feed bag.

"First the cemetery, then we'll put up for the night." He rode directly to the cemetery after asking directions from the man lighting the street lamps. Jackson followed the black painted sign nailed crooked to the oak tree, down the willow-shrouded lane.

The old stonecutter who lived on the grounds behind the line of trees heard him coming. "That hoss of yours looks rode hard."

"Come a long way. Need to borrow that lantern if you'd do me that."

"Awful late to be payin' respects."

"I won't be long."

Jackson went up and down the rows, scanning the graves, trying to find her name. Twinkling, sparkling broken glass—traces of kids doing what they shouldn't have been doing was everywhere.

"Place is a mess," he grumbled, unhappy that his daughter would spend eternity there.

When he took the lantern back, he did what he should have done first. "I'm looking for my daughter's grave. Her name's Darleda Jackson."

The gnarled old man with the bent and bony fingers didn't know anything about Darleda's grave. It wasn't on the records.

"I cut most every gravestone and marker out there," he said, waving his hand toward the graves as if they were his family.

"Could she have been put in the pauper section?"

"We don't got one here. Town puts everyone's name on a stone." The man went back inside his little house and brought out a musty book. "It'd be in the record book here. All the dead ones are listed as they come in. That's how I bill the folks for which stone went where."

"Check again. Please."

The caretaker double-checked. "Nope. I'd remember buryin' an orphan girl. Last one from the orphanage we put to rest here was Mr. Wilson. He's buried over yonder by the oak tree."

Bypassing the hotel, Jackson rode to the sheriff's office, hoping to get some answers. Sheriff Peterson was on the steps, closing up for the night.

"What can I do for you, stranger?"

"I'm tryin' to find my daughter's grave."

"At this time of night?"

Jackson was tired and began to ramble. "I don't have much time. My daughter died at the orphanage and was buried in the cemetery. I looked for the grave and couldn't find it. I got to make it back to the train depot near the Arkansas border and . . ."

"And hold on there. You're talkin' too fast. Start again. From the beginning."

Jackson did and when he was finished, Sheriff Peterson was puzzled. "I didn't hear nothin' 'bout any of the orphan girls dyin'."

"Here's the death notice I was sent," Jackson said, unfolding it.

Peterson looked it over. "Mister, there must be some confusion here. I talked to a girl named Darleda Jackson just a few hours ago. Ate dinner with her."

"You sure?" Jackson was feeling faint, hoping this wasn't a mistake.

"Positive. She gave me this to give to the Youngun boy."

Peterson showed Jackson the dime novel. Pointed out the message she'd written, thanking Larry. Signed by his daughter.

"Could you point me to the orphanage?" Jackson asked.

Sarah opened the door. The house moaned as the day heat evaporated off the walls. A little wind from over the ridge rattled the front windows, shaking the panes. Her eyes quickly adjusted to the dark hallway. A dust ball floated down from the doorjamb, hovering at eye level, then scooted sideways from the window draft.

Whoosh. Whoosh.

She opened and closed the scissors. Her head was throbbing. Her temples, her membranes calling out for relief.

Her husband lay in bed, worrying about the future. About what he should do, could do for Sarah. *She's sick. Gotta take her to the doctor tomorrow. Even if she doesn't want to. I've gotta do what's right for once.*

The floorboards creaked.

John lay still, wondering if it was just the old house groaning. He waited, counting the seconds, trying to see if his ears were playing tricks. The night sounds of the Ozarks were just outside the window.

They creaked again.

It's her. Sarah's sneakin' down the hall. For the first time in their marriage he was frightened. The blanket wrapped around him was no comfort. Made him seem vulnerable. He wanted to call out, shout out, but didn't, thinking that she might just be going to the kitchen for milk and didn't want to awaken him.

Soft footsteps moved toward his door. Then stopped, as if she too were waiting. The door slowly opened. Sarah entered, spotlighted by a moonbeam, the sharp, shiny scissors raised above her head.

John gulped, trying to sit up.

The blanket slid to the floor as she rushed toward him. He kicked at the nightstand, knocking it over. She tripped on the table leg, smashing it, throwing her aim off. John kicked again, knocking the air from her chest. She stood straight up, then plunged the scissors down into the pillow where his head had been.

He wrestled her down and grabbed for her arm, but the insanity gave her strength. She stepped back, than ran toward him screaming, aiming the scissors at his chest. "You'll pay, you'll pay!"

They writhed and rolled onto the floor, banging against the foot of the bed. The scissors dropped, lost to them both in the darkness. Sarah clawed at him, bit his ear. Her breath was foul, her eyes that of someone he didn't know. His arms ached but he couldn't let up. Whining, screaming, moaning, she bested him, smashing his head down onto the bed leg with a thunk.

Dazed, blood trickling down past his eyes, he watched her feel around for the scissors, yelping like a beast, talking, babbling, snarling, snapping. The blood trickled off his nose, over his lip, onto his shirt. "Sarah. Don't do this. Please."

Sarah tossed aside chairs, kicked at the bed, her mind set on finding the scissors. John saw them near his foot, and he nudged them under the bed.

"Where are they?" she growled.

"Stop it, Sarah!" he said, rising to lock his arms around her.

Moaning, growling like a beast, she kicked and punched him.

"Control yourself. Sarah, it's me. John, your husband."

He rolled on top of her and pulled the pillowcase free, to tie her hands with. She lay there breathing hard, glaring like a trapped animal, her eyes fixed with hatred. John pulled the knot hard.

"I'll go call the doctor," he said, thinking she had calmed down.

As he turned she kicked him in the small of the back, knocking him against the wall. He crumpled, almost unconscious, to the floor. Sarah used her teeth to undo the knotted pillowcase, then headed out the door.

"Sarah," he whispered hoarsely, the pain in his head almost blinding. "You gotta stop."

"I'm going to talk to Darleda," she smiled, "then I'm coming back to see you. I won't let you lock me away again."

54

Escape

❖

The lump on Darleda's head was purple. Just touching it made her feel like puking. There was no turning back. She was desperate to escape. The woman was crazy. She could have left already, but she wouldn't leave Little Jim. Jamming his clothes into the burlap sack she whispered, "Hurry, we don't have much time."

"Where we gonna go?" he said.

The future couldn't hold anything worse than the present. Darleda figured that the fact that they were going was more important than where they went.

"Maybe New York, anywhere, just away from here," she said.

"But he said that we'd start havin' fried chicken and . . ."

"That woman won't change. Somethin's wrong with her. I got a bad feelin' that if we stay here we're gonna die here."

"Did Mr. Robison tell you somethin'?"

"Nope. He didn't have to. I know she's two quarts short of a gallon in her head."

"Wish we had somethin' to protect us," he said.

"We do. We got nothin' else but prayers. But that's enough to get us where we're goin'."

Little Jim looked out the window, trying to find a shooting star among the sparklers. "We need us an angel. That's what I've been waitin' for."

"If an angel's comin', he'll find us. Let's go," she said, taking the frail boy's arm. It was dark outside. It would have been easier to escape in the morning, but Darleda was scared of what the night still held if they stayed.

Sarah saw them sneaking from the dorm, caught in the glow of the circle drive light. She recognized Little Jim by his limp. "Come back here!" she shouted.

The boy froze. "It's her!"

"Run. Quick," Darleda said, grabbing his arm. She had wanted to take one of the horses, but now it was too late. If they could make it to the woods then they might have a chance.

Sarah ran after them, obsessed with keeping the girl from escaping. "Darleda. Come back. I want to talk to you."

The children in the dorms began to moan and wail like alley cats.

Larry rode across the field. It was harder going in the dark, but he'd made good time. There wasn't much sense in trying to sneak in so he took the main entrance and rode toward the main building. He was determined to ride right up and tell Mr. Robison that he knew bad things were going on. That no one was going to hurt Darleda while he was around.

He found the door of the main house open. "Mr. Robison?" he called out. A breeze creaked by the door, moving it slightly. "Anyone home?" Goose flesh grew like hives on his arms. Something was wrong.

"In here. Help me."

Larry found Mr. Robison still dazed on the floor. "What happened, Mr. Robison?"

"Call for help," John said weakly.

"What happened?" Larry repeated.

"My wife. She's crazy."

"Where is she now?"

"Don't know. She ran off to find Darleda."

"Oh no," Larry whispered, standing up.

"Don't go after her, son, she'll hurt you bad."

The words were wasted, for there was no stopping the young knight.

❖ ❖ ❖

Little Jim kept tripping and falling. It was only a matter of time until Mrs. Robison caught up with them. "Leave me, Darleda, save yourself," Little Jim cried.

They heard the crazy woman scream out their names.

"Just keep runnin'," Darleda gasped, out of breath from dragging him along.

"Darleeeeeeeda!"

"Go," Little Jim whispered. "I'll hide under that tree there."

Mrs. Robison screamed out again. "Darleeeeeeeda! Where are youuuuuuuuuuuu?"

"Look for a rock, Jim. Find somethin' to fight with," Darleda said.

Darleda wasn't in the dorm. Neither was Little Jim. The kids Larry could find, who hadn't run off to hide in the barn, said that Mrs. Robison had gone after them. She had a knife or something in her hands and was calling out Darleda's name.

Larry heard the woman screaming and followed her voice. It was terrible knowing that he was tracking an insane woman who had just tried to kill her own husband. Now she was after Darleda. He picked up a stick to defend himself. It was all he could find.

He ran, tripping over stumps, bruising his hands, scratching his face on the low branches. By the old barn where he and Jim had buried the fawns, he saw them. Standing in the moonlight. Backs to the barn wall. Mrs. Robison was coming toward them.

"Oh Lord," Larry whispered.

The largest cougar he'd ever seen was atop the boulder not twenty feet away, pawing at the moonlight. Darleda saw the animal too. It was blocking their escape.

Robert Jackson found the orphanage entrance in the dark and rode in. His horse was half dead. White, crusted foam covered its lips. He should have switched horses in town, but there wasn't any time. His daughter was alive, that was all that counted.

Things weren't right. There wasn't a life to the place. It was dark. Foreboding. The horse's hooves echoed a life of their own.

"Anybody here?"

What he found scared him. Mr. Robison with a bleeding forehead, calling the sheriff, saying that his wife had gone crazy. Little children crying, hiding, begging him not to hurt them.

"Where's my daughter?" he asked the man.

"Your daughter?" Robison was weak from the loss of blood.

"Darleda. Darleda Jackson."

"You better go help her. My wife might try to hurt her bad."

"Where'd she go?"

"Somewhere in the woods."

Jackson ran off blindly. *Which way should I go?* "Darleda!" he shouted. Night birds mocked him. "Darleda!"

"She done gone that way," said a little boy peeking out from the dorm window. "Mrs. Robison was after 'em. They're gone suckers if you ask me."

The cougar roared.

Jackson went to his horse and took out his rifle, levered in a round and headed off, following the cat's roar and the scream of a girl. His daughter

Larry came toward Mrs. Robison, swinging the stick. "Go on back now. Leave them alone," he said.

Mrs. Robison hissed, then laughed. "Stay out of this," she said, raising her arms.

"Darleda, you take Little Jim and go on back to the orphanage. Call the sheriff."

Mrs. Robison stepped closer. The girl didn't move.

"You hear me?" Larry called out. "Take Little Jim and run. Now." He kept his eye on the cougar, which was moving closer and closer.

Then, without warning, the cat leaped toward him, claws extended. Larry braced for it, figuring he was dead. A shot rang out and the cougar buckled and bent in midair. The big cat fell at Larry's feet, muscles twitching. It was a clean shot to the head.

Larry turned and saw a strange man standing there in the moonlight. Little Jim whispered, "Darleda, it's my angel."

"Oh my word!" Darleda said, "it's Daddy!" She ran and wrapped herself around him.

Mrs. Robison started toward them. "Back off, lady," Jackson said, pointing his rifle toward her. He clicked in another round. "I don't want to hurt you, lady," he said, his emotions under control but trying not to make any sudden motions.

Darleda felt the air being sucked out of her lungs.

"I want Darleda," Sarah hissed.

Jackson stood his ground, his rifle locked vice-tight in his steady hand. "No. You ain't gettin' her no more."

Sarah blinked, breathing funny, like she was lost in a world of her own. Looking around, she moaned softly, then licked her lips like a woman burning up with fever. She turned and ran off into the woods, howling like a beast. The darkness absorbed her, swallowed her, like it was reclaiming one of its own.

"That woman's insane," Jackson said.

Jackson's words hung in the air.

"Where have you been?" Darleda whispered.

"She wrote me that you were dead, Darleda." Then he noticed her hair, and she started crying, telling him what had happened. "I'm sorry I didn't come sooner, honey. So sorry. I'll make it up to you in Denver, you'll see."

Larry watched, jealous for a moment. He felt like the third wheel on a bike. *Stop it. I'm bein' selfish,* he told himself, truly glad that she'd gotten her pa back. He wanted to call out to her as she walked arm in arm with her father, but the words wouldn't come. Little Jim started to cry, wondering what was going to happen to him now, believing that Darleda had forgotten her promise.

"You'll be all right, Jim," Larry said gently.

"But we were gonna be a family. Me and Darleda."

"There's a family out there for you. I know it."

"And I believed in angels," Jim mumbled, kicking at a dirt clump with his good foot. "They ain't real."

By the time the sheriff got there it was too late to mount a hunt for Mrs. Robison. "Boys," he said to his deputies, "you stand guard on the kids. We'll find that crazy woman at first light and cart her off to the bug house."

The deputies looked around without moving.

"You boys just got air between the ears? Get on back and watch them kids."

As they walked away the sheriff looked at the dead cougar and said to Larry, "There's your monster of the woods," he said, stooping down to look closer at the fangs.

"What about the chimp?" Larry asked. "Has anyone seen it?"

"You mean the ten-foot-tall, fire-breathin', flyin' dragon?" The sheriff laughed. "Everybody and his brother claims to have seen it. They'll be talking about Mud Monsters from here to kingdom come." He stood up and reached into his back pocket. "Darleda wanted me to give this to you," he said, handing Larry the dime novel.

Larry read the message Darleda had written and wanted to thank her. He walked with Little Jim back to the orphanage, barely able to keep from running ahead to find her. But Little Jim wouldn't even do a fast limp. Just walked along like a lost pup. By the time Larry got Jim back to his cot, Darleda was gone to stay at the hotel with her father.

While the sheriff did a fair job of bandaging up Mr. Robison, Larry sat on the edge of Little Jim's cot, waiting for him to fall asleep. The boy looked so frail, so sad, that it made Larry feel bad.

"Don't lose hope," he whispered. "Angels are real."

He left when Jim fell asleep. Riding alone, he felt older than his eleven years but wondered why things turned out as they did. The stars seemed brighter, like they were itty-bitty twinkling lampposts in heaven. *Angels?* He believed because he believed. *Denver?* He didn't even know where it was. Now she was gone, and he wondered if he'd ever see her again.

There was a lot to think about on the slow ride home. Eleven years of life was a short distance on the long road of life. Larry struggled to hold back the tears, glad that no one was there to see him cry. It wasn't what a knight should do, but he couldn't help it.

55

Candy Heaven

❖

Maurice and Billy had tried to follow Terry in the wagon, but they had to stick to the roads. The goat mobile was going helter-skelter over hill and dale.

"Them goats ever get tired?" Maurice asked.

"They can run a long time," Billy said.

"Think we better go to town and round up some help," Maurice said, clicking the reins.

They took the shortcut and made it to Mansfield just as the action began. Maurice barely had time to tie up the team when he heard the whooping and hollering. "Think we got trouble," he said.

Terry and Sweet careened into town, the forty-goat team completely out of control. Drunks scattered in the street doing a free-for-all do-si-do as the wagon spun past the saloon on two wheels.

"What the heck is that?" a farm boy shouted, pointing to the ape.

His friend shrugged. "Beats me. Looks like some kind of cowboy leprechaun and a dog-ugly fool."

Billy ran after them, waving his arms. "Sweet, it's me, Billy Goat Man."

Sweet cocked his head, like they shared a guilty secret, then hooted, flapping his arms, slapping his hands on the side of the wagon.

"Mr. Springer. Help me!" Terry called out to Maurice.

"Hold on, boy," Maurice answered.

"Help me, Mr. Springer!"

"Just don't let go."

Billy ran behind them, but the goats were still going full speed. "That's my wagon. Bring it back."

"Tell me how," Terry shouted.

The goats ran up and down the alleys, knocking over garbage cans, sending screeching cats looking for shelter. Dogs howled. People threw open their windows, wondering what all the ruckus was about.

The goats came up to the town square and started going around and around. Within minutes a crowd of gawkers had formed, scratching their heads, wondering if they'd ever see such a sight again.

Two dogs with big thoughts of goat dinners charged in, and the goats headed across the square, around the bandstand, through the shallow end of the pond and then clackety-clack down the wooden sidewalk with Maurice, Billy, and a dozen other men coming right behind.

"Help me!" Terry shouted.

"Hold on, we're gonna catch you," Maurice answered.

Sweet kept kissing and hugging Terry, covering the boy's eyes with his hands.

"Let go, let go!" Terry shouted. Then he saw it. They were on a dead-solid crash landing path. Bedal's store was smack dead ahead.

"Help me, Lord, I'll be good, I swear!"

The goats didn't turn. The wall was getting closer.

"Please God. I'll go to church. I'll really read the Bible. I don't want to be flattened like a bug."

They got closer.

Terry closed his eyes saying the fastest Lord's Prayer in history. At the last second the goats spun left. The wagon went two-wheels up, knocking Terry to the bottom. Sweet fell on top of him. The weight and strain broke the reins. The last thing Terry remembered was the wagon flying in the air. Right through the window. Crashing into the store.

When he came to, he thought he had died and gone to candy heaven. He was lying in a pile of sugar. Candy was everywhere. He didn't know that all the commotion outside was Maurice, Billy, and a dozen other men trying to catch the hyper goats who were heading every which way.

The chimp leaned over and hooted, showing Larry a mouthful of sour balls. Terry grinned and buried his face in fifty pounds of gumdrops.

"I always knew I'd go to heaven," he grinned, stuffing his mouth with more candy than he'd ever seen before.

56

Adoption Day

❖

I t took the town a week to really absorb what had happened. To come to terms with the bad things that had been going on. There weren't any Mud Monsters or boogeymen. Those were just tall tales. The real monsters were those who mistreated children, which brought the people to their senses. By the time Mrs. Wilson had come back for the Board meeting, the Methodist Ladies Aid Society had taken turns helping out at the orphanage and were planning the biggest Adoption Day that Mansfield had ever seen.

The Younguns gave Sweet another bath and doused him with smelly French perfume, which almost covered up the skunk smell. Sherry got her picture taken with the chimp, to prove she had really touched him. Henry Mead and Dr. George stood arm in arm with the chimp, for a newspaper picture to show they were good sports.

"Don't look ten foot tall to me, doctor," Mead winkea.

"Guess we both need glasses."

Billy was tickled about the Mud Monster stories but was sorry that Mead had lost his dog. Sweet didn't care much what anyone did to him. His stomach was so sore from the two hundred and eighty-two sour balls that he had gobbled down that he didn't even open his eyes when they flashed the big shadow box camera. The only thing that perked him up was the sweet potato pie that Eulla Mae baked up especially for him.

Before Billy Goat Man took Sweet back to the circus, he found a stray pup and gave him to Mead. "His name's Little Rufus." Billy winked, pushing Sweet up into the wagon. The chimp didn't put up a fuss. He just wanted to lie on the floor of the wagon, moaning from all the candy he had eaten.

Billy promised Mr. Bedal that he'd send him the money to repair his store just as soon as he got his reward from the owner of the circus for bringing the chimp back.

"Gonna call Sweet the Missouri Mud Monster. People will pay big bucks to see him." The crowd cheered as the forty-goat team pulled the strange little man and the hooting chimp out of town.

The sheriff took two men and found Mrs. Robison hiding in the woods the next morning. She came peacefully, hardly talking except for a few words here and there which didn't make much sense. Folks felt more pity than anger when they heard the whispers about her going crazy over losing her daughter.

Dr. George fixed up John Robison's head wound and locked Sarah in a room at the hotel until the train going to Louisiana came through. There was a special hospital down there, more like a church camp, which would let her live out her days there or stay until she got better, whichever came first. When they left town, Sarah sitting beside him with her hands strapped down tight, John Robison looked like the loneliest man in the world—he had a lot of hard nights ahead thinking about what never should have happened to the kids he'd promised to care for.

Rev. Youngun stayed out of the hoopla, recuperating in bed at the farmhouse. Eulla Mae stayed with him around the clock, feeding him her special soups and brewing up herb sun teas until he recovered. The kids did their best to help him get better, doing what Eulla Mae told them to, though Terry wasn't up to much. He still looked like he'd swallowed a basketball which was understandable, considering that he'd eaten two pounds of gumdrops by himself.

Larry did his chores, not talking much, wondering if he'd ever see Darleda again. The paper had said that Tippy had given her father the five-hundred-dollar reward for shooting the cougar, which Jackson used to buy passage for himself and Darleda to Denver. Larry looked at the grainy, black-and-white picture of her on the front page, standing with her father. "Off to Denver," he read. She was gone. Out of his life. Without even saying good-bye.

Maurice came up and sat beside him. "The heart's a funny thing," he began, "when Cupid first hits you with his arrow, it's a moment that you never, ever forget." He told Larry about the memories of young love that last forever. But it didn't make Larry feel any better. Only time would.

When Adoption Day came up the next weekend, Larry went to town with his family and the Springers to watch the ceremony. The Board had asked Mrs. Wilson and her sister to move back to Mansfield and they had agreed. The church meeting room was covered with colored paper, balloons, and streamers. Tables were piled high with cakes. Coffee was brewing. The church choir was humming in the corner getting ready to sing. Mrs. Wilson had a new sign made which she hung over the podium, "Rainbows for All God's Children."

Larry saw Little Jim standing off by himself. The other orphans were being pampered, primped, and pawed over. There were fresh haircuts, ribbons in the girls' hair. New clean shirts and pants were donated by Mr. Bedal. People were gawking at them and the orphans were looking around, hoping that they'd go to sleep that night as part of a real family.

"How come you're not over there with the others, Little Jim?" Larry asked.

The small boy scrunched his face, holding back a tear. "No one wants a crippled boy. You know that."

"There's a family somewhere for you. I know there is."

"I'm just waitin' for my angel."

Then they both saw her. Darleda was standing in the doorway, framed by beams of sunshine. Larry's throat went tight. His feet wouldn't move. He just stood there, watching her come closer, a smile wide and wonderful on her face. A moment he'd remember.

"I thought you were gone," he croaked, barely able to speak.

"Not without thanking my knight." She smiled. She leaned over and kissed his cheek and said into his ear, "I'll never forget you, Larry Youngun. Never, ever for the rest of my life. You'll always be my knight in shining armor."

He hated to ask but he had to. "When are you leaving?"

"In the morning. Going to Denver."

"Will you write?"

"Only if you write back," she grinned, squeezing his hand.

Little Jim turned away, covering his face with his hands, wanting to cry. She was leaving him. She'd promised to take him. That they would be a family. Now it was over and he'd never see her again.

"I hope you'll like Denver," Little Jim whispered through his hands.

"I hope you will too," she grinned, holding up a piece of paper with writing on it.

"What's that?" Little Jim asked, spreading his fingers wider so he could take a better look.

Darleda's father answered as he walked up. "That piece of paper says that you're my son. Shake my hand, Jim. I'm your father now."

Darleda began crying which got Larry to crying. Little Jim was already crying, and the whole thing made Robert Jackson and most of the folks in the room misty-eyed.

"Guess angels are really real," Little Jim said, gripping his new father's hand.

Mud Monsters, boogeymen. Those are make-believe stories to whisper around campfires. To put goose bumps up and down your arms. But angels, they're real. You can bet your life on it.

There are also earth angels, the good folks who reach out with their hearts to help others. Lending a hand. Taking someone into their home. Like Little Jim. His angel had come. He was part of a family now. Like all children should be.

Turn the page
for an excerpt from

Thomas L. Tedrow's

Shipwrecked on Cannibal Island

Book Five
Younguns series

Captured
by the
Headhunters

"**A**re they gonna eat us, Pa?" Larry asked.

Rev. Youngun was too exhausted to answer. It was all he could do to shield Sherry from the sun. She hadn't spoken in two days, her lips so cracked and parched that she seemed barely alive.

Five days at sea in the small whaling boat seemed a cruel fate. To go from shipwrecked to the salvation of sighting land, only to wonder now if they would be eaten, was agonizing.

"Tell me, Pa. Do you think they're the headhunters that the Captain told us about?"

"I hope not, son."

"Hope they don't like redheads," Terry grumbled, peeking over the side. It was his nightmares come to life. The stories that he'd heard on the boat about the headhunters of the Solomon Islands were now paddling toward him.

Larry clutched his pocketknife, fingering the blade. It felt small compared to the fight that was coming. "What should we do, Pa?"

"All we can do is pray."

Terry stared at the South Pacific natives paddling toward them in their canoe-like boats. "I don't like the looks of those spears."

"Maybe they're not going to hurt us," Rev. Youngun said quietly.

What had started as a family adventure was now a disaster. Rev.

Youngun's mission assignment to China had taken them from the safety of Mansfield, Missouri, to the edge of death. All he knew was that the ship had been blown off course in the storm and they were somewhere near New Guinea. Far away from America.

About the Author

❖

Thomas L. Tedrow is a best-selling author, screenwriter, and film producer. He prides himself on writing stories that families can read together and pass on to friends. He is the author of the best-selling eight-book series The Days of Laura Ingalls Wilder, the eight-book series The Younguns, and such new classics as *Dorothy— Return to Oz, Grizzly Adams & Kodiak Jack,* and other books and stories. Tedrow lives with his wife, Carla, and their four children in Winter Park, Florida.

Don't miss any of the exciting adventures of

THE
YOUNGUNS

Keep up with the kids who can't seem
to stay out of trouble.
Larry, Terry, and Sherry Youngun
get into mischief like bees into honey
yet cherish honesty, compassion,
courage, and kindness.